Ripples

Ricky Dragoni

Ripples by Ricky Dragoni

A Ricky Dragoni Publication/April 2017

This is a work of fiction. All names, characters, and incidents are the product of the author's imagination. Any resemblance to real person, living or dead, is entirely coincidental.

Published by
Ricky Dragoni

Printed in the United States of America

Ricky Dragoni

HUNTING GHOSTS

My boots clicked on the pavement as the gentle midnight drizzle fell on my leather jacket. My hips swayed in my tight black jeans and my Ramones t-shirt covered my chest. My long dark hair gave me a little shelter and warmth from the cold rain. I was heading to the same dive bar I had visited for the past 12 nights. The Sea Urchin, they never closed, but don't be surprised if your server is a prick. The building stood by itself. It looked like it had once been a house, fell on hard times, and ended up being gutted and made into a bar. The illuminated sign upfront was an undistinguishable black sea urchin with a light blue background. No one could ever tell what it was. Everyone made the same mistake of asking the bartender about the sign, who happened to be the owner as well. Mike, the owner, would berate them, insult them, and point out how uncultured and stupid they were for asking. After he was done with his rant and the customers sat there with a wide-eyed look, he would give them a free shot of whiskey and all was forgiven.

Unlike those naïve patrons, I had found my way here on purpose. I had sat and used every ounce of charm and flirtatiousness I had to lure him in. I wasn't here to get yelled at by Mike, I was here for a much bigger fish. I think tonight's get up and pouty lips might finally get him to make his approach. I sat at the end of the bar sipping on my rum and coke. He was at his usual table carefully scoping his possible victims. I knew how dangerous he really was and I should have felt afraid. I didn't. This wasn't my first rodeo and I had bagged creeps way more dangerous than him.

He wore what was left of his suit. His tie and jacket were gone and the neck of his fancy dress shirt was opened down a couple of buttons. He drank his usual water with lemon, the only reason Mike served it to him was because he would leave a $100 dollar tip for him. He was perfectly shaven with all too perfect skin. His hair was trimmed short on the sides and long

1

on top. It was combed and held immobile with some expensive product. I watched him through the mirror behind the bottles behind the bar. He didn't seem to fit in amongst the shady cast of The Sea Urchin, but not even the bearded bikers playing pool seemed to want any piece of him.

He sat there sipping on his water and oozed a dark energy which seemed to keep all the tables around him empty. His name was Patrick Michelson, no one knew about him yet, but when his exploits were finally exposed he would end up with 26 kills to his name. By my estimations he was just getting started, with maybe 2 or 3 victims so far. I needed to make sure he picked me next. I needed to erase him from the record.

I asked Mike for another rum and coke, he gave me a nod, and the drink appeared in front of me in his hand. He threw his bar towel over his shoulder and walked away to take care of other patrons who were holding onto the bar for balance. While Mike made and served my drink, Mr. Michelson had walked his way over to me like a lion stalking his prey. I had finally caught his eye. He approached me from my left, thinking I hadn't seen him.

"Put that on my tab, Mike." His voice was deep and manly. It rolled out of his mouth silky and velvety. His eyes were fixated on me as he said it. Mike nodded and kept going on his way. I pretended to be startled, jumped, and let out a little yelp. Didn't want to disappoint Mr. Michelson, he had worked so hard to try to catch me by surprise. After my academy award winning performance, I met his gaze and gave him a sensuous smile.

"Thank you Mr....?"

"Call me Pat. And you would be?" As he said it, he looked me up and down soaking in every inch and every curve of mine.

I extended my hand to him, following old and forgotten customs. "I am Jordan, pleasure to meet you, Pat." I smiled and bit my lower lip. He followed my lead, grabbed my hand and kissed it without breaking eye contact.

I invited him to sit with me. He kept buying me drinks, complimenting me, and seemed to be so interested in listening and learning everything he could about me. After a couple hours and eight or nine more rum and cokes, he finally tried to make his move. I knew if I gave in too easy he would not go over the edge with me and try to make me his next victim. He was now holding me between his arms and I coyly avoided giving my full eye contact; only looking at him out the top of my eyes, while keeping my head tilted down to avoid his attempts at kissing me.

"You should let me take you somewhere nicer than this, Jordan. Why don't we get out of here? We can continue this back at my place."

I could feel, much more than see, Mike scoff at Mr. Michelson's implication that this was not a fine establishment. I held back the sudden urge to smile at Mike's annoyance and shook my head gently, while biting my pointer finger. Mr. Michelson kept insisting, but I used my charm to get out of his arms and his invitation. I excused myself to the bathroom and pretended to stumble all the way there. Out of view from my predator I smiled, straightened my walk, passed the bathroom doors, and left The Sea Urchin through its back door.

I had him hooked. Now I had to let him simmer and become obsessed. Plus, I had other engagements to keep. Martha was ready to act and I could not very well leave her hanging. I walked down the dark ally. The dumpster behind The Sea Urchin smelled like it had been harboring a decomposing body for weeks. The puddles left from the cold rain made a field of land mines for my black leather boots. I avoided every one of them and reached the main street. It took me 20 more minutes of walking, but I made it to the Pink Mohawk. I walked past the heavily tattooed and bearded bouncer and was greeted by the loud music.

The mass of humanity jumped and thrashed around, filling the air with the smell of sweat and spilled beer. The band on stage played accelerated rifts while its lead singer spat half his words out into the microphone. The crowd became more violent as the drummer beat on the drums with the furor of a mad man. Even though the words where unintelligible, the crowd echoed every single sound.

I spotted Martha hanging on the bar desperately searching the crowd. Her eyes spotted what they had been looking for, probably for hours, me. I strode over to her as she gently bobbed her head to the angry beat coming from the stage. I looked at her and gave her my best Casanova smile. Her eyes brightened at my acknowledgement, while her mouth gave me a wide toothy smile. Her gaze broke from me for a second, just to turn around and yell something at the wide-eyed bartender. Those poor bartenders didn't seem to last long here.

By the time I had finished my short gander over to Martha, she had a beer bottle in hand, and a million caresses ready for me. She handed me the beer and clung on to me like a marooned sailor hangs on to a life raft.

"Where have you been, baby? I have been waiting for you all night." The way she looked at me was almost fanatical. I had interjected myself as target number four for dear Martha. She was in her early forties and still trolling the punk bars for willing and easy prey. She would only claim 11 if she kept going, but the ripples she created in the male consciousness truly reverberated.

If left to her own devices, she would not only kill eleven men, she would dismember them, and adorn her trophy room with their desiccated genitalia. She was one of the crucial seeds that snuck in and rooted itself for the victimhood of males for centuries to come. Those seeds would lead to me and that had to be stopped.

"Sorry babe, I was out spreading a little anarchy and tagging some pigs' cruisers." The moment I said it, her knees became visibly weak. Her eyes glazed and I could feel the utter lust emanating out of her. I had played my bad boy act well with her and she wanted nothing more than to make me her next trophy, little did she know. I chugged the beer she had provided and could taste the extra little bit she thought she had slipped past me in it.

"Let's go back to my place Jordan, make me yours." As she said it, I could see part of her was desperate for my acceptance and need. Part of her was so lost and so disconnected that I could almost see the monster behind her eyes. I knew she was ready and primed to act. It was my chance to erase her from the record.

I threw my beer bottle at the wall shattering it into hundreds of tiny little pieces. She squeezed me harder at the sign of my rebellion. I grabbed her by the hand and led her through the masses of bodies thrashing to the music and out the door into the cool night. We walked to her car. I got in and threw my boot up on the dash. She shivered visibly, composed herself, and drove off into the night with me, her prey. As we drove I found a good rock station, turned it up as loud as I could, and gave her more of what she wanted. I was a bad boy and she was going to fix me. At least that is how she justified it in the interviews with the police. We left the city and plunged into the monotony of suburbia. The wild 40-something punk wannabe lived in an upper middle class suburban house.

After wandering through the cookie cutter rows of houses, she slowed down as a garage door opened to our left. She turned and hid the car in its little alcove.

"We are here, baby. I am going to take care of you like no one ever has, Jordan." The first little bit of ugliness snuck out of her as she said it. I played the part she expected. I got out of the car, adjusted my crotch, spit on the spotless garage floor, and stumbled after her. She led me up three short steps out of the garage and into a perfectly decorated and manicured home. I helped myself into her fridge, found a beer, and proceeded to chug it for her benefit. Her hands were all over my chest and back until they finally found their way to my backside. She squeezed my ass, kissed me, and finished the kiss with a lingering nibble of my lower lip.

She led me up the carpeted stairs to her bedroom. As soon as we walked in I pushed her against the wall holding her arms by her wrists above her head. I pinned her with my body and started to kiss down her neck. I found my way to the base of her neck with my kisses. Once there I plunged my teeth into her soft white skin. A moan escaped her mouth and her knees buckled. I held her up against the wall by her wrists as she melted in front of me.

Martha was a very beautiful woman. She was still a looker for her age and you could tell that she had been truly beautiful once, back in her day. She had never had kids, being left infertile after contracting a STD during a gang rape while in college. She had kept her shit together through medication, counseling, and a supportive husband she had met years later. After 15 years of marriage, her supportive husband was no more. He left her, exhausted of dealing with her. Alone and left to stew in a pile of shit life had piled high on her, she finally snapped.

She had been hunting now for four years. Her descent into madness was a slow and methodical one. She had taken to hunting younger men; carefree, screw the world attitude kind of men, the same type who had scarred her for life. I must admit I felt bad for her, but once she flipped, there was no going back. She was a victim of circumstances, but her victims and her legend had helped shape a world I was hell bent on erasing.

She freed herself from my grip and turned me against the wall. Her eyes had turned feral, and before I ended up her trophy, she was going to enjoy ravishing me. Her eyes kept penetrating into mine as she lowered herself down to her knees. She gave one last look and turned her attention to my belt buckle and black jeans. She swiftly undid my leather belt and her eager fingers found her way to my jean button and zipper. She slowed down while undoing the button of my jeans, savoring every teasing moment. She slowly lowered the zipper and pulled down the jeans.

Her eyes widened as she stumbled backwards and onto her butt. She kept looking back and forth between my exposed crotch and my eyes. By now I had dropped the drugged and confused act. My eyes were cold and knowing. She saw the wisdom in my eyes and knew I saw her for the monster she truly was.

"What... What the hell is this? Is this a joke? Where? How? What the..?" I had pulled up my pants so I could move and rushed her in her confusion. My legs straddled her waist and I used my body to pin her down. She could no longer move; her terrified and confused eyes stared back up at me as she lay on her back.

As with all the others, I felt the need to apologize for what I had to do. "I am sorry, Martha." My hands found their way to her delicate neck. I squeezed as her eyes looked back into mine, not as a predator now, but as prey. Her hands helplessly fought to pry mine away from her only access to air. Her blonde hair framed her face as tears started to well in her blue eyes. As the tears fell they left a black line down her face, dragging with them the excessive amounts of black makeup. She struggled and thrashed against me, even trying to reach my face to push me away. Our eyes stayed locked the whole time and I saw the acceptance of what was happening in her eyes. She kept fighting, but she knew there was no escape. I looked into her eyes as they started to glaze over slowly, her face turning from red to purple and her chest struggling for short, or any kind of, breaths under my body. Eventually, her hands stopped fighting. Her mouth stayed open, hoping to catch any oxygen. Her eyes were still fixated on mine and I saw the light go out. I held my grip on her neck for a few more seconds to make sure she would not come back. Once I was satisfied her eyes were completely empty, I let go of her soft, delicate, and now bruised neck.

I took a second to remind myself why I was doing this and why I must do it. Finding my center and composure, I proceeded to give poor Martha an honorable goodbye. I gently picked up the sad and lonely woman. The wrinkles around her eyes and mouth were more noticeable now. I was careful as I picked her up from the carpeted floor. I gently placed her on her bed, covering her with the quilt draped on the bottom of her king sized bed. I took one last look into her beautiful blue eyes, gave her a kiss on her forehead, and closed her eyelids gently with my fingers. I lit all the candles I could find in her bedroom and she seemed to have several. I opened her bottom drawer and found the bottle of vodka she would drink herself to sleep with. I sprinkled some of the vodka over her lifeless body and around the room.

I stood next to her and took in how beautiful and broken she really was. I picked up the candle on the night stand next to her. I lit it with her lighter and watched the flame dance on her body.

"Thank you, Martha." Those were my last words to her as I gently let the candle slip out of my hand and on to Martha's body. The flame quickly found the quilt and the vodka, setting Martha ablaze. I walked out of the room as I tipped over some of the other candles I had previously lit. I stood at the doorway making sure the fire would take. Once I was satisfied with the raging flames inside the room, I turned and found my way out of the burning house.

The flames spread quickly, and by the time I had found my way to a safe distance, the blazes were engulfing the whole second story of the house. When the firefighters finally made it, the whole house was a burning inferno. In the flames that night, Martha and her legend were erased.

HELLO LOVE

Lumi most definitely will be visiting me soon. I am curious to know what ripples I erased. Until then, I had one more target, Mr. Michelson.

I made my way out from the prying eyes of the crowd that had gathered to watch the edifice burn. It took me a while to weave my way out of the suburban maze, but after much trial and error I achieved it. I finally spotted a cab and caught a ride back to my temporary home.

The cab dropped me off in front of an apartment building. Around it and next to it, were other buildings with storefronts on the lower levels and living quarters above them. I had secured myself a nice apartment for a change. My mission was what mattered; but I will admit, it is nice to have decent accommodations every once in a while. The doorman greeted me and opened the door for me. I walked across the white marble floors to the elevator. I climbed into the vertical carriage and number 23 illuminated after I pushed it. I looked down at the floor and waited for the "ding" to tell me I had arrived. Martha was still in my mind and I could not yet tolerate seeing my reflection on the elevator door.

I stood there quietly until the notice of the elevator set me into action. The doors opened in front of me and the hallway welcomed me. I took a right and found my way towards the door with 2399 on it. I opened the door and as I had suspected, Lumi was waiting for me sitting on the love seat.

Lumi was as beautiful as I was, actually exactly as beautiful as me. Lumi sat legs crossed, arms draped over the side of the loveseat, and gave me that priceless smile. Something looked different since the last time I had seen Lumi. By the time I had figured out what was different, I was deep in the embrace of a hug from Lumi. Being so out of time it was nice to see a familiar face.

"Your shoulders are wider old friend," I commented on the change as

7

my hands moved across my old friend's stronger shoulders.

"Well I wouldn't know, you know that trouble maker." Lumi looked at his shoulders trying to find the difference I saw, but ended up shrugging shoulders when no change was noticed. "I hadn't noticed, thank you for mentioning it. I take it you erased another one?"

"Yes, this one was harder than most. She never had a chance, but she needed to be erased." Martha's cold empty eyes flashed in my mind's eye as I tried not to think of tonight's events while catching Lumi up. Lumi nodded, seeing the pain in my eyes, and as always proceeded to say just the right thing.

"They are looking for you, trouble maker. You might be lost in the grid, but they are not stupid, you know this. Eventually someone will catch up with what you are doing." Ah... nothing like getting back to business.

Lumi and I were partners. Not in the sense humans were meant to be partners, but in the only way we knew how. We cared about each other. Lumi worried about what I was doing, realizing eventually enough attention will come to me that it might cost me my life. I was scared of it as well. Not of the dying, but not achieving what I needed to do. It was still nice to know I had someone in my corner and worried about me.

"I know. Hopefully, I can cause enough ripples before they do. I need to know what being human means. We... I don't know what we are, Lumi." Lumi gave me a soft smile and nodded, agreeing with my madness or genius.

"Well I will say this; I didn't expect 2020 to still be this slimy and dirty. You would think we would have had our shit together by this century. How many more targets do you have left, Jordan?" Lumi could not help being mortified and disgusted at the living conditions of our species. It always amused me, I was the one wading through it, but Lumi was the one disgusted by it.

"One more that I have identified, Patrick Michelson." The moment I said the name, Lumi's eyes opened wide recognizing it. Lumi's hair was a much lighter shade than mine and really contrasted with the black leather couch. It wasn't quite blonde, but as close as brown can get to blonde. Lumi's parents chose it during the design process. There was still some customization in the process to provide the appearance of individuality, but it was all superficial. Seeing Lumi's hair and wide beautiful hazel eyes refocused me on what I needed to do.

Lumi instantly recognized the look, having seen it hundreds of times. The smile on Lumi's face still melted me and it spread across the beautiful face. "Well, I wanted to let you know, so far so good. But please be careful." Lumi stood from the black leather love seat and strode towards me. I wish I could have felt the need I had seen in people's eyes as I walked towards them that minute. The walk was graceful, sensuous, and assertive. Lumi's body was now pressed against mine and as our succulent lips met I wished I could feel more things, deeper and more intimate. Sadly, neither of us could. I yearned for the day when we both would.

After the eternal kiss, Lumi took a step back, punched a few buttons on the armband, and was gone. I stood in the fancy apartment alone and felt frustrated I didn't feel alone. The pink and oranges in the sky outside the window were starting to announce the impending coming of the sun. It was time for me to get some rest. I found my way through the classically decorated apartment to the bedroom. I found the king size bed, stripped down naked, crawled under the blankets, and went to sleep.

Two hours later I was awake. The clock on the nightstand read 8:22 AM. Two hours exactly, every night, another of the great advancements of genetic engineering. I yearned for the night I would experience my first dream. I had read and researched them, but never had the pleasure to experience one myself. They were deemed unnecessary and even harmful. So of course, like everything else that might have adverse effect, they were eliminated. I lay in bed a few more seconds staring at the red numbers of the alarm clock. I wished I felt anything else, but awake and invigorated. Unfortunately, that is all I could feel at the moment, so I got up and found my way into the shower.

I didn't quite need it, but the warm water always felt so great against my skin in the morning. The hot water turned the bathroom into a sauna and I had to clean off the mirror over the sink to see myself after my scalding shower. My hair hung heavy from my head and my face seemed to pop through it. That is when the little, but important detail, caught my eye. Unlike Lumi, my shoulders hadn't grown wider, at least I didn't think so. That was a good sign. I hoped it was real.

I got ready this time in a stylish grey two piece suit and went out into the crisp morning to do a little more research on Mr. Michelson. An expensive suit gets you a cab pretty quick and I made my way to the financial district. It was obvious we were getting closer, since all the people navigating the wide sidewalk wore an infinite array of greys and suits. Once we hit Wes Jackson Boulevard, the cabby asked me where I wanted to be dropped off. I pointed to some random corner and told him there was good. As he expected, I paid my fare and left a large tip. Amazing how monetary exchange was still so important in this time.

I exited the cab once it came to a stop and entered the busy street navigated by power suits, preoccupied faces, and cell phone conversations. Everyone on the sidewalks seemed to be a in a hurry to get somewhere which wasn't there. Eye contact was elusive if non-existent at best, since everyone was either talking into a phone or navigating through. I stood there and let the masses of strangers walk around and past me. A smile would decorate my face when one of the bustling pedestrians would actually catch a glimpse of me and stare as they walked. Their mouths would hang open as they stared and soaked in my symmetry and beauty. I decided to move when one of the businessmen ran into a light post trying to keep his eyes on me, while giving me a silly grin.

I walked a couple of blocks north until in front of me a very stylish concrete building extended up to the skies. The law firm in which Mr. Michelson was a novice partner, resided on the 13th floor of the building. I knew I would not be able to work my way past security and onto his floor, but I had found lobbies can be such an informative place. I bought a newspaper from the dispenser on the corner and made my way into the building.

I walked confidently and no one seemed to question me belonging there. It was close to ten, so I knew Mr. Michelson would be arriving soon. I found my way into one of the uncomfortable, but fashionable chairs in the lobby and hid behind my newspaper. There was a big terracotta pot next to me which housed a giant peace lily. I could not resist choosing that spot, I was so fascinated by the large plant diversity that still existed. Right on cue, Mr. Michelson broke the threshold of the lobby and strode confidently through it. He smiled and greeted a few people on his way to the elevators, but he was all business.

He was a very successful criminal defense lawyer and it was that knowledge and skill which had kept him free to kill and maim as he pleased. I wanted to follow him up to his office. I wanted to dig deeper into his world and what made him tick. I needed that knowledge to help me with the others.

As I sat there, I could barely focus. The feel of the newspaper in my hands was overwhelming and distracting. Organic matter pressed and dried. Its smell was unique and I could not help to associate it with death. The feel of it between my fingers was fantastic. I would rub my thumbs and pointer fingers and enjoy the feel of the paper between them. It was surprisingly complex. At first it felt smooth, but as the tips of my fingers dug deeper I could feel the imperfection and its roughness.

As I sat there mesmerized and distracted by the feel of the paper between my fingers, Mr. Michelson disappeared. I kept trying to deny it, but what my touch really yearned for was Lumi's skin. Seeing Lumi the night before had me beyond distracted. It had been too long since I was able to fall asleep in the same bed with Lumi.

I decided it was futile to keep fighting it. I rolled up the sleeve of my suit and dress shirt to expose my navigation armband. I made a note of the precise place and second, set my destination for home, and I was gone.

I was back in my chair inside the grey concrete room. The chair was our version of leather, which, from my travels, I now knew was nowhere close to the real thing. The computer turned itself from monitoring mode to active mode the second I was back in the room.

"Welcome back, Jordan. Hope your mission was a success." Although life-like, the voice still was off. After all these years of technology and advancement, computer voices still didn't quite sound completely human.

"Thank you, TX92. Yes, the trip was very successful." Of course AI TX92 wasn't talking about the same mission I was on. Even with all their powerful computer intellect, they could still be fooled. I stood up from the faux leather chair and approached the terminal. I carefully uploaded all the information I had collected from 2020, making sure none of the other adventures were communicated.

I was a temporal scout. My career and my life had been engineered to travel through time, observe, and upload data to the mainframe. There were many of us, our collective information determined what time and places would be safe for time tourist to visit. The information was also used to expand on the historical record. Advanced scouts would be sent to critical and important moments in time in search for the truth, but never interfering. I was but a Basic, so I had decades to go until I made it into Advanced.

The protocol was always to observe and never to interfere. A couple of advanced scouts in the 700 years of the programs had forgotten that directive. They were made into examples. Death would have been a welcome relief for what they had to go through. I knew what I was doing was even graver, but I was determined to see it through. I finished loading up, said goodbye to TX92, and left the plain concrete box which was my office.

The heavy metal door unlocked as I approached it and allowed me to escape into the sun filled hallway. The building for KronoCorp was circular and all the scout's offices filled its circumference. It made it so when we walked out of our scouting mission, the first thing that welcomed us was the city, and our time outside the full length glass windows.

I was lucky; outside my office I had an amazing view. I could see the San Francisco channel and across from it North America. KronoCorp was located on the island of San Andreas and had become the time traveling center for the world. I soaked in the view for a few seconds then proceeded to the elevator which rode down the center of the glass building.

Once the vault of an elevator had delivered me down to the lobby, the anticipation of getting home and seeing Lumi crept into me. With purpose in my steps, I made short work of the large lobby. Unlike many of the timelines I had scouted, style served no real purpose anymore. The lobby was as spectacular as my concrete box of an office. There was no need to adorn the inside, all the true beauty was outside, and provided free by nature. All buildings followed this rule, simple, clean, and an outer shell made of glass to provide views of outside.

I exited into the bustling street. It was like I was in suburbia, but instead of the houses looking the same, it was us that did. Everyone was beautiful, was baked in the same oven, and completely androgynous. Every time I returned from scouting missions and I exited into the masses in the city, I was reminded how generic and boring I really was. Everyone seemed to find me fascinating and beautiful in my travels. Here I was just another boring loaf of bread baked in the same mold as everyone else.

I set that feeling aside and joined the human traffic like a good little sheep. I followed the crowd into the subway station. As I walked amongst the mass of people, identical buildings as KronoCorp flanked me on both sides. They differed in height and even size, but every building was a cylindrical shell of glass, housing every type of business and purpose. I reached the stairs of the subway and followed them underground.

I stood on the platform along with a couple hundred people. Like every other structure, it was plain grey concrete devoid of any adornments. The distant noise of the air being displaced in front of the subway started to resonate in my ears. I could not yet see it, but I could tell it was approaching from the tunnel on the left. As the distant light on the front of the subway began to shine out of the darkness, I could feel the magnetic track start to charge. The hairs on the back of my neck stood in attention and my ears began to pop. Transportation authorities keep arguing that any prospective passengers reporting symptoms like that were just under stress. The symptoms were supposedly caused by their own anxiety over riding the subway. I knew what I was feeling and I was certain the large electromagnetic field that was preparing to stop the subway was the cause. I knew there was no harm in it, but I didn't understand why they insisted on lying to the people.

The solid metallic worm exited out of its hole and came to a stop in front of the waiting mass of people. As the doors opened they made a swishing sound. From the opening emerged a batch of perfectly beautiful and manicured "individuals". Everyone looked different, but yet the same. The main differentiation between them was the length and color of hair, along with what they wore. They didn't see it. They were regular people like the other two billion on the planet and the millions off-world.

My eyes and my perception changed after my 17 scouting missions. Until then, the people I got to observe were primitive, weak, and a vestigial remnant of the past. During that mission, whether by coincidence or destiny, I saw the most beautiful thing my two perfect eyes had ever seen. The year was 1979, I was scouting the birth of Punk music in the late 20th century. The births of every great music movement seemed to be a great time traveling destination. Punk, because of its violent and revolutionary birth and nature, had to be thoroughly scouted prior to tourists being allowed to experience it. One too many scouts had been injured in mosh pits. KronoCorp kept searching for safe points to introduce the tourist.

On my way to one of the New York underground punk concerts is where my eyes opened. I was riding a very antiquated and primitive version of a subway. Across from me an elderly couple sat holding hands. I could not tell what their age was, but what little hair they had was either white or grey. They held on to each other's hands, their boney fingers covered in loose and wrinkly skin interwoven lovingly. Every time the subway made a jolt or quick movement, the gentle old woman's hand would grip tighter on the man. Her white hair looked like a poufy cloud resting on top of her tired head. Her dress was a dark brown with random patters of pink and other colors speckling it. She clutched on to her oversized brown purse as if her life depended on it. She stared into the nothingness of her memories and swayed back and forth with the subway. The old man wore a hat which had seen its fair share of rain and sunshine. His face hid under it adorned by a big bushy white mustache. Wrinkles and spots adorned his clean shaved cheeks. He sported a black suit with a tie to go along with it. Wherever they were going, it was a formal occasion as his carefully shined black shoes showed.

They were everything technology had worked so hard to avoid. At that moment I felt nothing but pity and a little disgust towards them. The old man caught me staring at them, grabbed the tip of his hat with his right hand and smiled at me. I smiled back at him, doing my best to hide my true feelings towards them. I had been trained for moments like these. We scouts got to see a lot of the ugly underbelly of our species past.

The primitive subway came to a stop and apparently the old couple and I were sharing the same exit. I doubted they were going to the same punk music concert I was going to, but we were disembarking in the same exit nonetheless. The old man pried himself off the seat and was trying to help his wrinkly bride up. I went around them and exited onto the platform. I was well on my way to the stairs out into the streets when something made me turn. Still to this day I don't know what it was, but the urge to turn was so strong I could not fight it.

I stopped my graceful steps and did a turnabout, framed perfectly between two graffiti covered pillars of the platform, stood the old couple. The slow old man was helping along his even slower partner. She walked with a bit of a hunch and her hand shook as he helped her along by the arm. They stopped as she uttered something I could not make out from a distance. They faced each other and I could see his left profile and her right. They both smiled while staring into each other eyes. Her shaking hands came to a rest in his and they stood there smiling at each other like teenagers. She tilted her head up as their faces approached each other. Their lips puckered as their eyes still smiled at each other. Lips met and they held each other. In that moment, something flipped inside of me.

Their once ugly wrinkles became beautiful years together. Their slow walk was but the tired walk of two souls who had lived so much together. Their old and tired shells evaporated and I could see what they really were. They were still two silly teenagers madly in love with each other. That kiss, that night, that couple made me realize how beautiful they truly were and what we had become in our search for perfection. When I returned from that scouting mission all I could think of was how Lumi and I would never get to grow old together like that beautiful couple in the subway station. It broke me inside, and every time I come back to the ugliness of our perfect beauty, it disgusts me a little more.

The mass of ugly perfection was done exiting the subway so I boarded and could not wait to get home to Lumi. I stared into oblivion during the subway ride and remembered that beautiful kiss and why I had to do, what I had to do. The ride ended, I walked out of the metal worm, out of the station, and into the street. The masses bustled up and down the street. I found my walking flow lane and headed to my place. The outside here was identical as the previous; a myriad of cylindrical glass buildings of variant heights. After centuries of engineering, a perfect building was attained, now the streets of every metropolis and city were littered with them.

I finally found my way to my housing building and entered it with great anticipation. I found the metal box of an elevator and pressed floor 33 and upwards I went. Concrete, glass and metal was all my world was, all for the sake of uniformity and practicality. Everything held the same muted and clean tone, except for what beauty nature provided us. Well that was the case until I entered my apartment. Pictures of sunsets, bridges, hillsides, people, and events decorated the walls; all drawn by me and allowed by Lumi. I had even learned how to make my own pigments, so the grey concrete walls held splashes of color and things I had seen.

To my disappointment, the well decorated apartment was empty. I shook it off and went to take a well-deserved shower. The hot scalding water felt great on the back of my head and body. The nozzles sprayed my naked body from every direction. I had to admit it was nice to be home. The glass fogged over and the room filled with a cloud of steam. I closed my eyes and all I could see were the eyes of those I had erased staring back into my soul. My conviction never wavered, but I wondered if it was all a fool's errand. The time and space continuum could be such a tricky thing.

Suffocating in the steam, I prompted the bathroom to turn the exhaust fan on. The steam quickly cleared and I exited the shower. I dried myself and went into the bedroom to look for a new change of clothes. After much debate I settled into some comfortable pajamas. I wasn't planning on going anywhere for the rest of the day. I navigated my way into my favorite comfortable faux leather chair and enjoyed the views outside the apartment windows.

The hive looking city of cylindrical glass buildings sprawled in front of me. Eventually the cylinder glass buildings gave way to the San Francisco channel. The waters were turquoise even from a distance. The channel was close to 4,000 years old. The Yellowstone mega volcano started the cascade. After the third major eruption all the major faults went crazy. The San Andreas Fault finally had enough and created the island in which I now work and reside. The shallow sea between the San Andreas Island and North America was one of the most beautiful in the world.

The island was completely devastated and, with impending and frequent follow up earth quakes and aftershocks, it stood desolate for almost 500 years. The only people frequenting the island were scientists studying the unique and extreme ecological experiment which Mother Nature had left on their laps for them. Nature took over, eating through concrete, returning the land to its original form. The first human outpost was established in 3,251. As always we explored, then moved in like a parasitic plague and re-established our presence in the land. The files from that era look nothing like the island looks now in 6,749. The island was now the nerve center of technology and no natural green spaces were left. The only green spaces were engineered, designed and executed to perfection by the government. The only natural thing left was the stunning aqua marines of the channel.

I stared at the millions of shades of blue and green getting mixed by the waves until my trance was interrupted by the opening door. I tried to contain my excitement of running to the door to greet Lumi, but failed miserably. My feet were possessed and by the time the door closed behind Lumi, I was already embracing the delicious body in front of me. I kissed Lumi with my lips and soul and wished I felt but an ounce of what I had seen in that old couple. Lumi's lips felt amazing against mine, but that was it. Nothing stirred, nothing melted, and my smile was full of sorrow. As always, Lumi looked at me as if I were crazy.

"Well hello to you too Jordan, didn't expect to see you here." The expression quickly turned into a charming and welcoming smile. I snuggled into Lumi's chest in search of something that sadly didn't exist. The strong arms embraced me and for a second, I pretended.

"I missed you. It was futile, I could not focus, I needed this." I mumbled the words, still cuddled in the strong chest. The feeling of foolishness started to creep into my gut and I broke the embrace. Lumi still smiled at me, but I knew this journey was a lonely one.

That night, after a satisfying dinner, I fell asleep next to Lumi and knew my visit had to be a short one. If I wanted to make more than a ripple, I still had an enormous amount of work to do. The belief in the butterfly effect is greatly overestimated. Yes, changing a big historical event in the past will have large repercussions in the future. But destiny seems to find a way to correct the errant path of its chaos. After enough time passed, small changes seem to get lost in the totality of it all. I had to make enough small undetectable changes that still added up to a large change; all of it without getting caught while working. I think I had it figured it out, but only time will tell as it always does.

I fell asleep that night wondering if it was worth it. I woke up the next morning even more determined than ever. I enjoyed a wonderful breakfast with Lumi and we both headed into KronoCorp. Lumi to follow his determined time scouting missions, me to figure out how to proceed with my own agenda. No hands were held in our walk and no kiss goodbye graced my lips. I knew Lumi loved me, but after seeing what love could be, I wished I could receive that from my beautiful partner. I shook it off and proceeded to find my way to my concrete office.

THE CHASE

Lumi most definitely will be visiting me soon. I am curious to know what ripples I erased. Until then, I had one more target, Mr. Michelson.

I made my way out from the prying eyes of the crowd that had gathered to watch the edifice burn.   It took me a while to weave my way out of the suburban maze, but after much trial and error I achieved it. I finally spotted a cab and caught a ride back to my temporary home.

The cab dropped me off in front of an apartment building. Around it and next to it, were other buildings with storefronts on the lower levels and living quarters above them. I had secured myself a nice apartment for a change. My mission was what mattered; but I will admit, it is nice to have decent accommodations every once in a while. The doorman greeted me and opened the door for me. I walked across the white marble floors to the elevator. I climbed into the vertical carriage and number 23 illuminated after I pushed it. I looked down at the floor and waited for the "ding" to tell me I had arrived. Martha was still in my mind and I could not yet tolerate seeing my reflection on the elevator door.

I stood there quietly until the notice of the elevator set me into action. The doors opened in front of me and the hallway welcomed me. I took a right and found my way towards the door with 2399 on it. I opened the door and as I had suspected, Lumi was waiting for me sitting on the love seat.

Lumi was as beautiful as I was, actually exactly as beautiful as me. Lumi sat legs crossed, arms draped over the side of the loveseat, and gave me that priceless smile. Something looked different since the last time I had seen Lumi. By the time I had figured out what was different, I was deep in the embrace of a hug from Lumi. Being so out of time it was nice to see a familiar face.

"Your shoulders are wider old friend," I commented on the change as

17

my hands moved across my old friend's stronger shoulders.

"Well I wouldn't know, you know that trouble maker." Lumi looked at his shoulders trying to find the difference I saw, but ended up shrugging shoulders when no change was noticed. "I hadn't noticed, thank you for mentioning it. I take it you erased another one?"

"Yes, this one was harder than most. She never had a chance, but she needed to be erased." Martha's cold empty eyes flashed in my mind's eye as I tried not to think of tonight's events while catching Lumi up. Lumi nodded, seeing the pain in my eyes, and as always proceeded to say just the right thing.

"They are looking for you, trouble maker. You might be lost in the grid, but they are not stupid, you know this. Eventually someone will catch up with what you are doing." Ah... nothing like getting back to business.

Lumi and I were partners. Not in the sense humans were meant to be partners, but in the only way we knew how. We cared about each other. Lumi worried about what I was doing, realizing eventually enough attention will come to me that it might cost me my life. I was scared of it as well. Not of the dying, but not achieving what I needed to do. It was still nice to know I had someone in my corner and worried about me.

"I know. Hopefully, I can cause enough ripples before they do. I need to know what being human means. We... I don't know what we are, Lumi." Lumi gave me a soft smile and nodded, agreeing with my madness or genius.

"Well I will say this; I didn't expect 2020 to still be this slimy and dirty. You would think we would have had our shit together by this century. How many more targets do you have left, Jordan?" Lumi could not help being mortified and disgusted at the living conditions of our species. It always amused me, I was the one wading through it, but Lumi was the one disgusted by it.

"One more that I have identified, Patrick Michelson." The moment I said the name, Lumi's eyes opened wide recognizing it. Lumi's hair was a much lighter shade than mine and really contrasted with the black leather couch. It wasn't quite blonde, but as close as brown can get to blonde. Lumi's parents chose it during the design process. There was still some customization in the process to provide the appearance of individuality, but it was all superficial. Seeing Lumi's hair and wide beautiful hazel eyes refocused me on what I needed to do.

Lumi instantly recognized the look, having seen it hundreds of times. The smile on Lumi's face still melted me and it spread across the beautiful face. "Well, I wanted to let you know, so far so good. But please be careful." Lumi stood from the black leather love seat and strode towards me. I wish I could have felt the need I had seen in people's eyes as I walked towards them that minute. The walk was graceful, sensuous, and assertive. Lumi's body was now pressed against mine and as our succulent lips met I wished I could feel more things, deeper and more intimate. Sadly, neither of us could. I yearned for the day when we both would.

After the eternal kiss, Lumi took a step back, punched a few buttons on the armband, and was gone. I stood in the fancy apartment alone and felt frustrated I didn't feel alone. The pink and oranges in the sky outside the window were starting to announce the impending coming of the sun. It was time for me to get some rest. I found my way through the classically decorated apartment to the bedroom. I found the king size bed, stripped down naked, crawled under the blankets, and went to sleep.

Two hours later I was awake. The clock on the nightstand read 8:22 AM. Two hours exactly, every night, another of the great advancements of genetic engineering. I yearned for the night I would experience my first dream. I had read and researched them, but never had the pleasure to experience one myself. They were deemed unnecessary and even harmful. So of course, like everything else that might have adverse effect, they were eliminated. I lay in bed a few more seconds staring at the red numbers of the alarm clock. I wished I felt anything else, but awake and invigorated. Unfortunately, that is all I could feel at the moment, so I got up and found my way into the shower.

I didn't quite need it, but the warm water always felt so great against my skin in the morning. The hot water turned the bathroom into a sauna and I had to clean off the mirror over the sink to see myself after my scalding shower. My hair hung heavy from my head and my face seemed to pop through it. That is when the little, but important detail, caught my eye. Unlike Lumi, my shoulders hadn't grown wider, at least I didn't think so. That was a good sign. I hoped it was real.

I got ready this time in a stylish grey two piece suit and went out into the crisp morning to do a little more research on Mr. Michelson. An expensive suit gets you a cab pretty quick and I made my way to the financial district. It was obvious we were getting closer, since all the people navigating the wide sidewalk wore an infinite array of greys and suits. Once we hit Wes Jackson Boulevard, the cabby asked me where I wanted to be dropped off. I pointed to some random corner and told him there was good. As he expected, I paid my fare and left a large tip. Amazing how monetary exchange was still so important in this time.

I exited the cab once it came to a stop and entered the busy street navigated by power suits, preoccupied faces, and cell phone conversations. Everyone on the sidewalks seemed to be a in a hurry to get somewhere which wasn't there. Eye contact was elusive if non-existent at best, since everyone was either talking into a phone or navigating through. I stood there and let the masses of strangers walk around and past me. A smile would decorate my face when one of the bustling pedestrians would actually catch a glimpse of me and stare as they walked. Their mouths would hang open as they stared and soaked in my symmetry and beauty. I decided to move when one of the businessmen ran into a light post trying to keep his eyes on me, while giving me a silly grin.

I walked a couple of blocks north until in front of me a very stylish concrete building extended up to the skies. The law firm in which Mr. Michelson was a novice partner, resided on the 13th floor of the building. I knew I would not be able to work my way past security and onto his floor, but I had found lobbies can be such an informative place. I bought a newspaper from the dispenser on the corner and made my way into the building.

I walked confidently and no one seemed to question me belonging there. It was close to ten, so I knew Mr. Michelson would be arriving soon. I found my way into one of the uncomfortable, but fashionable chairs in the lobby and hid behind my newspaper. There was a big terracotta pot next to me which housed a giant peace lily. I could not resist choosing that spot, I was so fascinated by the large plant diversity that still existed. Right on cue, Mr. Michelson broke the threshold of the lobby and strode confidently through it. He smiled and greeted a few people on his way to the elevators, but he was all business.

He was a very successful criminal defense lawyer and it was that knowledge and skill which had kept him free to kill and maim as he pleased. I wanted to follow him up to his office. I wanted to dig deeper into his world and what made him tick. I needed that knowledge to help me with the others.

As I sat there, I could barely focus. The feel of the newspaper in my hands was overwhelming and distracting. Organic matter pressed and dried. Its smell was unique and I could not help to associate it with death. The feel of it between my fingers was fantastic. I would rub my thumbs and pointer fingers and enjoy the feel of the paper between them. It was surprisingly complex. At first it felt smooth, but as the tips of my fingers dug deeper I could feel the imperfection and its roughness.

As I sat there mesmerized and distracted by the feel of the paper between my fingers, Mr. Michelson disappeared. I kept trying to deny it, but what my touch really yearned for was Lumi's skin. Seeing Lumi the night before had me beyond distracted. It had been too long since I was able to fall asleep in the same bed with Lumi.

I decided it was futile to keep fighting it. I rolled up the sleeve of my suit and dress shirt to expose my navigation armband. I made a note of the precise place and second, set my destination for home, and I was gone.

I was back in my chair inside the grey concrete room. The chair was our version of leather, which, from my travels, I now knew was nowhere close to the real thing. The computer turned itself from monitoring mode to active mode the second I was back in the room.

"Welcome back, Jordan. Hope your mission was a success." Although life-like, the voice still was off. After all these years of technology and advancement, computer voices still didn't quite sound completely human.

"Thank you, TX92. Yes, the trip was very successful." Of course AI TX92 wasn't talking about the same mission I was on. Even with all their powerful computer intellect, they could still be fooled. I stood up from the faux leather chair and approached the terminal. I carefully uploaded all the information I had collected from 2020, making sure none of the other adventures were communicated.

I was a temporal scout. My career and my life had been engineered to travel through time, observe, and upload data to the mainframe. There were many of us, our collective information determined what time and places would be safe for time tourist to visit. The information was also used to expand on the historical record. Advanced scouts would be sent to critical and important moments in time in search for the truth, but never interfering. I was but a Basic, so I had decades to go until I made it into Advanced.

The protocol was always to observe and never to interfere. A couple of advanced scouts in the 700 years of the programs had forgotten that directive. They were made into examples. Death would have been a welcome relief for what they had to go through. I knew what I was doing was even graver, but I was determined to see it through. I finished loading up, said goodbye to TX92, and left the plain concrete box which was my office.

The heavy metal door unlocked as I approached it and allowed me to escape into the sun filled hallway. The building for KronoCorp was circular and all the scout's offices filled its circumference. It made it so when we walked out of our scouting mission, the first thing that welcomed us was the city, and our time outside the full length glass windows.

I was lucky; outside my office I had an amazing view. I could see the San Francisco channel and across from it North America. KronoCorp was located on the island of San Andreas and had become the time traveling center for the world. I soaked in the view for a few seconds then proceeded to the elevator which rode down the center of the glass building.

Once the vault of an elevator had delivered me down to the lobby, the anticipation of getting home and seeing Lumi crept into me. With purpose in my steps, I made short work of the large lobby. Unlike many of the timelines I had scouted, style served no real purpose anymore. The lobby was as spectacular as my concrete box of an office. There was no need to adorn the inside, all the true beauty was outside, and provided free by nature. All buildings followed this rule, simple, clean, and an outer shell made of glass to provide views of outside.

I exited into the bustling street. It was like I was in suburbia, but instead of the houses looking the same, it was us that did. Everyone was beautiful, was baked in the same oven, and completely androgynous. Every time I returned from scouting missions and I exited into the masses in the city, I was reminded how generic and boring I really was. Everyone seemed to find me fascinating and beautiful in my travels. Here I was just another boring loaf of bread baked in the same mold as everyone else.

I set that feeling aside and joined the human traffic like a good little sheep. I followed the crowd into the subway station. As I walked amongst the mass of people, identical buildings as KronoCorp flanked me on both sides. They differed in height and even size, but every building was a cylindrical shell of glass, housing every type of business and purpose. I reached the stairs of the subway and followed them underground.

I stood on the platform along with a couple hundred people. Like every other structure, it was plain grey concrete devoid of any adornments. The distant noise of the air being displaced in front of the subway started to resonate in my ears. I could not yet see it, but I could tell it was approaching from the tunnel on the left. As the distant light on the front of the subway began to shine out of the darkness, I could feel the magnetic track start to charge. The hairs on the back of my neck stood in attention and my ears began to pop. Transportation authorities keep arguing that any prospective passengers reporting symptoms like that were just under stress. The symptoms were supposedly caused by their own anxiety over riding the subway. I knew what I was feeling and I was certain the large electromagnetic field that was preparing to stop the subway was the cause. I knew there was no harm in it, but I didn't understand why they insisted on lying to the people.

The solid metallic worm exited out of its hole and came to a stop in front of the waiting mass of people. As the doors opened they made a swishing sound. From the opening emerged a batch of perfectly beautiful and manicured "individuals". Everyone looked different, but yet the same. The main differentiation between them was the length and color of hair, along with what they wore. They didn't see it. They were regular people like the other two billion on the planet and the millions off-world.

My eyes and my perception changed after my 17 scouting missions. Until then, the people I got to observe were primitive, weak, and a vestigial remnant of the past. During that mission, whether by coincidence or destiny, I saw the most beautiful thing my two perfect eyes had ever seen. The year was 1979, I was scouting the birth of Punk music in the late 20th century. The births of every great music movement seemed to be a great time traveling destination. Punk, because of its violent and revolutionary birth and nature, had to be thoroughly scouted prior to tourists being allowed to experience it. One too many scouts had been injured in mosh pits. KronoCorp kept searching for safe points to introduce the tourist.

On my way to one of the New York underground punk concerts is where my eyes opened. I was riding a very antiquated and primitive version of a subway. Across from me an elderly couple sat holding hands. I could not tell what their age was, but what little hair they had was either white or grey. They held on to each other's hands, their boney fingers covered in loose and wrinkly skin interwoven lovingly. Every time the subway made a jolt or quick movement, the gentle old woman's hand would grip tighter on the man. Her white hair looked like a poufy cloud resting on top of her tired head. Her dress was a dark brown with random patters of pink and other colors speckling it. She clutched on to her oversized brown purse as if her life depended on it. She stared into the nothingness of her memories and swayed back and forth with the subway. The old man wore a hat which had seen its fair share of rain and sunshine. His face hid under it adorned by a big bushy white mustache. Wrinkles and spots adorned his clean shaved cheeks. He sported a black suit with a tie to go along with it. Wherever they were going, it was a formal occasion as his carefully shined black shoes showed.

They were everything technology had worked so hard to avoid. At that moment I felt nothing but pity and a little disgust towards them. The old man caught me staring at them, grabbed the tip of his hat with his right hand and smiled at me. I smiled back at him, doing my best to hide my true feelings towards them. I had been trained for moments like these. We scouts got to see a lot of the ugly underbelly of our species past.

The primitive subway came to a stop and apparently the old couple and I were sharing the same exit. I doubted they were going to the same punk music concert I was going to, but we were disembarking in the same exit nonetheless. The old man pried himself off the seat and was trying to help his wrinkly bride up. I went around them and exited onto the platform. I was well on my way to the stairs out into the streets when something made me turn. Still to this day I don't know what it was, but the urge to turn was so strong I could not fight it.

I stopped my graceful steps and did a turnabout, framed perfectly between two graffiti covered pillars of the platform, stood the old couple. The slow old man was helping along his even slower partner. She walked with a bit of a hunch and her hand shook as he helped her along by the arm. They stopped as she uttered something I could not make out from a distance. They faced each other and I could see his left profile and her right. They both smiled while staring into each other eyes. Her shaking hands came to a rest in his and they stood there smiling at each other like teenagers. She tilted her head up as their faces approached each other. Their lips puckered as their eyes still smiled at each other. Lips met and they held each other. In that moment, something flipped inside of me.

Their once ugly wrinkles became beautiful years together. Their slow walk was but the tired walk of two souls who had lived so much together. Their old and tired shells evaporated and I could see what they really were. They were still two silly teenagers madly in love with each other. That kiss, that night, that couple made me realize how beautiful they truly were and what we had become in our search for perfection. When I returned from that scouting mission all I could think of was how Lumi and I would never get to grow old together like that beautiful couple in the subway station. It broke me inside, and every time I come back to the ugliness of our perfect beauty, it disgusts me a little more.

The mass of ugly perfection was done exiting the subway so I boarded and could not wait to get home to Lumi. I stared into oblivion during the subway ride and remembered that beautiful kiss and why I had to do, what I had to do. The ride ended, I walked out of the metal worm, out of the station, and into the street. The masses bustled up and down the street. I found my walking flow lane and headed to my place. The outside here was identical as the previous; a myriad of cylindrical glass buildings of variant heights. After centuries of engineering, a perfect building was attained, now the streets of every metropolis and city were littered with them.

I finally found my way to my housing building and entered it with great anticipation. I found the metal box of an elevator and pressed floor 33 and upwards I went. Concrete, glass and metal was all my world was, all for the sake of uniformity and practicality. Everything held the same muted and clean tone, except for what beauty nature provided us. Well that was the case until I entered my apartment. Pictures of sunsets, bridges, hillsides, people, and events decorated the walls; all drawn by me and allowed by Lumi. I had even learned how to make my own pigments, so the grey concrete walls held splashes of color and things I had seen.

To my disappointment, the well decorated apartment was empty. I shook it off and went to take a well-deserved shower. The hot scalding water felt great on the back of my head and body. The nozzles sprayed my naked body from every direction. I had to admit it was nice to be home. The glass fogged over and the room filled with a cloud of steam. I closed my eyes and all I could see were the eyes of those I had erased staring back into my soul. My conviction never wavered, but I wondered if it was all a fool's errand. The time and space continuum could be such a tricky thing.

Suffocating in the steam, I prompted the bathroom to turn the exhaust fan on. The steam quickly cleared and I exited the shower. I dried myself and went into the bedroom to look for a new change of clothes. After much debate I settled into some comfortable pajamas. I wasn't planning on going anywhere for the rest of the day. I navigated my way into my favorite comfortable faux leather chair and enjoyed the views outside the apartment windows.

The hive looking city of cylindrical glass buildings sprawled in front of me. Eventually the cylinder glass buildings gave way to the San Francisco channel. The waters were turquoise even from a distance. The channel was close to 4,000 years old. The Yellowstone mega volcano started the cascade. After the third major eruption all the major faults went crazy. The San Andreas Fault finally had enough and created the island in which I now work and reside. The shallow sea between the San Andreas Island and North America was one of the most beautiful in the world.

The island was completely devastated and, with impending and frequent follow up earth quakes and aftershocks, it stood desolate for almost 500 years. The only people frequenting the island were scientists studying the unique and extreme ecological experiment which Mother Nature had left on their laps for them. Nature took over, eating through concrete, returning the land to its original form. The first human outpost was established in 3,251. As always we explored, then moved in like a parasitic plague and re-established our presence in the land. The files from that era look nothing like the island looks now in 6,749. The island was now the nerve center of technology and no natural green spaces were left. The only green spaces were engineered, designed and executed to perfection by the government. The only natural thing left was the stunning aqua marines of the channel.

I stared at the millions of shades of blue and green getting mixed by the waves until my trance was interrupted by the opening door. I tried to contain my excitement of running to the door to greet Lumi, but failed miserably. My feet were possessed and by the time the door closed behind Lumi, I was already embracing the delicious body in front of me. I kissed Lumi with my lips and soul and wished I felt but an ounce of what I had seen in that old couple. Lumi's lips felt amazing against mine, but that was it. Nothing stirred, nothing melted, and my smile was full of sorrow. As always, Lumi looked at me as if I were crazy.

"Well hello to you too Jordan, didn't expect to see you here." The expression quickly turned into a charming and welcoming smile. I snuggled into Lumi's chest in search of something that sadly didn't exist. The strong arms embraced me and for a second, I pretended.

"I missed you. It was futile, I could not focus, I needed this." I mumbled the words, still cuddled in the strong chest. The feeling of foolishness started to creep into my gut and I broke the embrace. Lumi still smiled at me, but I knew this journey was a lonely one.

That night, after a satisfying dinner, I fell asleep next to Lumi and knew my visit had to be a short one. If I wanted to make more than a ripple, I still had an enormous amount of work to do. The belief in the butterfly effect is greatly overestimated. Yes, changing a big historical event in the past will have large repercussions in the future. But destiny seems to find a way to correct the errant path of its chaos. After enough time passed, small changes seem to get lost in the totality of it all. I had to make enough small undetectable changes that still added up to a large change; all of it without getting caught while working. I think I had it figured it out, but only time will tell as it always does.

I fell asleep that night wondering if it was worth it. I woke up the next morning even more determined than ever. I enjoyed a wonderful breakfast with Lumi and we both headed into KronoCorp. Lumi to follow his determined time scouting missions, me to figure out how to proceed with my own agenda. No hands were held in our walk and no kiss goodbye graced my lips. I knew Lumi loved me, but after seeing what love could be, I wished I could receive that from my beautiful partner. I shook it off and proceeded to find my way to my concrete office.

DAY 1

The streets were buzzing, not figuratively, but literarily. Everyone was out, it was the middle of the night and the streets were covered with excited and mostly drunk Chicagoans. The police were out in force also, but the celebrations were peaceful and joyful. Eventually, the police and even the rivaled South Siders, joined in the celebration. They knew it was history they were part of. I tried to focus and study for further missions, but the excitement outside was too much. I gave in and decided to join the masses. Walking down the still dark streets, everyone was sporting smiles and carrying their preferred libations.

It should have descended into chaos, anarchy, and rioting, but the monumental achievement seemed to keep everyone in a happy disposition. That was the reason we were scouting this event, I was strolling through what was going to become a 4 day celebration and a 21st century joyous orgy.

As I listened to the masses sing celebratory hymns and continue in the drunken celebration, I could not help myself and found myself smiling; it was truly infectious. I strolled my way through the celebration on the streets and before I knew it The Sea Urchin was in sight. I didn't expect Mr. Michelson to have found his way here during the celebration, but The Sea Urchin had become familiar to me, so I decided to go in and celebrate.

I was overwhelmed by the excitement now and felt like one of the locals. I broke the crest of the entryway and my smile quickly vanished from my face. To my dismay, Mr. Michelson was trolling The Sea Urchin. Instead of broodily sitting in his desolate table, he was hanging all over a poor blonde woman wearing a Cubs jersey. His charm was turned up to 11 and the poor gal looked like a drunken moth heading for the light.

She was a pretty girl in her early 20's. Her sandy blonde hair was pulled up in a ponytail held tight by a blue scrunchie. She wore a pinstriped white

Maddox jersey, showing she was a hard core fan. Her makeup was minimal and she still looked beautiful. Her face held that fullness that no cream or product can ever provide. She smiled and hung on every word Mr. Michelson spewed to her. She stood and headed for the bathroom and revealed her height. She was tall and slender and couldn't help herself from looking back to see if Mr. Michelson was looking at her walk. He didn't disappoint and smiled at her when she turned her head. Her feet seemed to become bouncier as she finished her stroll to the ladies room.

The Sea Urchin was a big bar, but it still held its dark and secluded corners. I worked my way to a booth where the lights didn't work and Mike hadn't bothered to fix them. The table was still covered in beer bottles and a few drink glasses. I hid behind them and pretended I was their owner. I watched and waited.

The blonde finally came out of the ladies room still with the same bounce in her step, but now also wearing a sensuous shade of red lipstick. People were buzzing all around her and she never saw them. Her dilated eyes were fixated on only one thing, Mr. Michelson. He watched his prey willingly walk towards him. He pulled her in tight to his body and whispered something in her ear. Her knees visibly buckled for a second, whether at what he said or his breath in her ear I don't know, but they did. She frantically nodded at his offer as her smile widened showing teeth. Mr. Michelson grabbed his prey by the hand and they weaved their way through people and out of The Sea Urchin.

I watched through the front window in what direction he took her. I waited a few seconds, left my booth, and followed from a safe distance. They walked so close, tangled in each other's arms, I didn't know how they didn't trip and fall. I felt exposed and thankfully, a passed out drunk on the sidewalk provided a little cover. The large man was sitting on the sidewalk slumped over against a store front. Like many of the people littering the streets, he was wearing all of his Cubs gear, including a hat. I grabbed the man's hat, placed it on my head, and felt a little more shielded from Mr. Michelson's eyes. The baseball cap was a little too big, but I made it work and continued in my stealthy pursuit.

We were heading east and every street and every intersection were abuzz. As they walked, you would think there was a bubble around them. He kept leading her in a straight line and the people celebrating automatically moved out of their path. The orange colors in the horizon were starting to make the presence of the approaching sun down. He was heading to the lake for a sunrise walk. What girl could resist?

Once we reached the shore line of the lake, following them without getting noticed became a little more challenging. He chivalrously helped her down to the water's edge and they began the walk along the lake as the waves gently lapped at their now bare feet. His left and her right hand were an interwoven mess of fingers. The other hands held their respective shoes; their faces were all smiles and blushing. It was an extremely sweet and romantic scene, but I knew there would be no happy ending to this story.

I pulled down the bill of the cap a little more to hide from Mr. Michelson's searching eyes. I kept my distance, so their eyes could not see me clearly, but I could clearly see them. As expected, he finally stopped and they exchanged a very passionate and intense kiss. Shoes were dropped and searching hands explored each other's bodies. The sun was no longer an impending certainty, it was now a reality on the horizon, and its rays framed and warmed them in their passionate embrace. The kiss broke and her eyes were still closed as he searched around for secluded and private place. He whispered what must have been dirty words into her ear, because her now open and feral eyes bore into him as her head agreed.

A wave breaker flanked by a sand dune was their destination. By the time I reached them and used the concrete fingers of the wave breaker as seclusion, the moans and noises of skin slapping against skin filled the air. I carefully peeked around the concrete pillar and saw them in the heat of passion. She had been liberated of her jersey and other garments and laid naked on her back on top of the sand. Her hands and fingers reached upward as if trying to find something to grip and rip from her intense pleasure. Mr. Michelson's muscular arms flanked her face as his hips thrust between her spread legs. Her moans became screams and pure gibberish exited her mouth and she reached her climax. He didn't stop; his face was neutral, as he didn't appear to be enjoying the experience.

His hands shifted from resting on the sand to exploring the delicateness of the blonde's neck. The muscles on his arms and naked chest rippled as his grip on her neck went from playful to serious. Still hypnotized by the dance of his hips between her legs, the blonde just went along with it and actually appeared to be enjoying the new game Mr. Michelson was playing. Her moans once again became louder, her fingers dug into the sand, and once more she reached her climax. The hands didn't stop pressing on her neck and her moans had left her lungs devoid of any air. His eyes were focused on her face and were full of excitement. His mouth gave away a thin smile making his whole expression sinister and dark. His muscles strained harder to deprive the now panicky blonde of any air.

I felt compelled to intercede, but I wasn't the victim, I couldn't. If I saved her from him I would have to erase her myself. I could not let her live, I would be mentioned in the record, and everything I had been working so hard and quietly for, would be revealed. I could not save her and I could not kill the innocent blonde. I did the only thing I could....watched.

Her once blissful face was now engulfed in fear and panic. Her hands reached up in desperation towards Mr. Michelson's face. Her arms, being much shorter than his, failed her and all she could do was scratch and claw at his muscled shoulders. His smile had now grown to a full teeth baring snarl and his eyes were dilated and possessed. His hips kept thrusting harder and harder, in and out of his struggling victim. The moans that filled the air were now replaced by small almost inaudible struggling noises. Tears begun to run down the sides of the blonde's face as every gulp didn't deliver much if any air into her lungs. Her arms slowed down and eventually crumpled next to her. She kept looking up at him and the tears streamed down her face. Her body gave up the fight and went completely limp. His grip intensified on her neck, his body convulsed, and his expression became savage. He stayed there locked in his ecstasy as the poor blonde lay dead beneath him.

Once done, he stood up and started to cover his naked body with his fancy and expensive clothes. The blonde's body lay like a discarded condom on the sand. Pants and shirt on, he did a quick surveying of the shore line looking for possible curious eyes. I avoided his search and continued to watch his methods unfold. He piled all the girl's clothes in a nice little pile. He pulled some hand sanitizer out of his pants pocket and emptied the tiny bottle onto the dead girl's garments. Out of his other pocket, he pulled a small roll of what appeared to be twine. The incredibly small, but long bundle of twine allowed him to tie the girl's neck, then a loose piece of large concrete from the wave breaker, then her feet. His precision was admirable. His calm demeanor was impressive and chilling. He placed the piece of concrete on top of the girl's stomach and dragged her by her feet to the lake. He pulled her in until he was shoulder high in the surf; her lifeless body gently bobbing on the small waves.

Once he had reached his target depth, he tipped the small boulder of concrete off her stomach. Her body flipped leaving her exposed backside up and began to sink. Once satisfied that the body would not float back up, he exited the lake, his clothes drenched in cold lake water. Mr. Michelson walked back to his last string to tie the pile of clothes. He grabbed the box of matches he had left next to the pile, opened the box and retrieved one match carefully, so as not to get it wet. He struck the match on the side of the box and used it to light the whole box of matches. The sulfuric smell filled the air. He threw the flaming box of matches on the pile of the girl's clothing. It lit up and blazed furiously as he extended his hands towards the flames for warmth. Between the alcohol in the hand sanitizer and the rubber in the girl's shoes, the flames were furious.

I should have left, I should have interceded, but all I could do was watch this madman kill and dispose of his victim. The clothes were now almost a pile of flaming ashes, so Mr. Michelson started his walk back toward the city. I watched him as he increased the distance between my hiding spot and him. His walk was confident; there was not an ounce of guilt or nervousness in his body. He looked like a man just going for a stroll down the lake. He climbed up a dune and disappeared into the city. I found it prudent and safe to leave now, so I started to make my way back towards the celebrating city and my quiet apartment.

Half way back to the apartment I changed my mind and, being morning, went into a diner for some breakfast. I sat down, still numb from what I had seen. During the whole ordeal, time had slowed down and I got to soak in every drop of sweat and every tear that was shed. I knew Mr. Michelson was a monster; what really bothered me was if that was what I transformed into when I erased my targets. The waitress dropped off my order and brought me out of my thoughts. The diner was filled with hung over Cubs fans and she didn't have time for pleasantries. She rushed off to the next demanding and obnoxious table in her section.

Outside the diner the streets were still buzzing. A new batch of fans that had either woken up to the news or were on their second wind, were scattered throughout the streets. The steel cans with four wheels were barely moving as traffic was at a standstill from all the pedestrians celebrating. I left the chaos outside and focused on the stack of three pancakes sitting in front me. The assortment of syrups rested inside of sticky individual dispensers lined along the wall on the booth's tabletop. I carefully inspected the sugary treats and decided on a combination of peach, blueberry, and maple. Time travel does have its benefits of tasting things that were no longer available. I lifted the pancakes and drowned each spongy morsel with a different flavor, finishing with maple over the top. The pancakes sat in a pool that they would quickly absorb. I dove in with my fork and knife and forgot about all missions, sanctioned or my own clandestine agenda. They were delicious.

Satisfied and with an overload of sugar trying to make my heart beat out of my chest, I dropped a few $100 bills on the table for my pancakes and coffee. I walked out of the diner and, as the glass door closed, I could hear the yelping of the tired and overworked waitress. She smiled as she made sure the bills were real. I really didn't quite understand the excitement these paper notes brought out of people. I knew not everything was free and accessible as in my time, but... anyways.

I kept walking and the crowd, now filled with coffee, was gaining momentum. Uniformed police officers hovered, making sure the celebration remained as peaceful as it had been so far. The masses of people were flowing in the same direction and curiosity forced me to follow along. The crowd kept converging and the mass of people growing. They all headed in the same direction as if they were being called by some subsonic siren. The grumble of voices grew as we approached the unknown destination. I got swept up by the excitement and before I knew it, found myself on Navy Pier along with the crowd. Songs echoed throughout the noise. Several of them competed and their melodies fought and worked with each other. It was a sea of blue and white with speckles of red breaking the mosaic pattern of the crowd. The vendors were open and selling bottles of beer as fast as their hands would allow them.

Again the uniformed cops stood in vigil and did nothing to discourage either the illegal alcohol selling or the celebration. Everyone was happy, many were drunk, and none were causing trouble. It was truly one of the most amazing things I had seen. Crowds like this lend themselves to violence and rioting. This crowd, this city, was celebrating a true historic event. I had time to kill. I joined in on the celebration and experienced the closest feeling a human could feel to a hive mind.

By midday a lot of the crowd had cleared the pier. The sun was beating down on them and already dehydrated from alcohol, they sought refuge from the sun. That didn't mean the celebration was over. Bars, restaurants, and hotel lobbies were inundated by the celebrating mass, just to find more people to join them. I decided I had enough of the experience and started to fight my way back to the apartment.

As the day wore on, the people celebrating were wearing less and less clothes. Toplessness, both male and female, was becoming rampant. The uniform wearing gargoyles watched the mass, and as long as no serious crime was being committed, their minor offenses were ignored. The crowd roared and cheered, especially when the females decided to share their mammary glands with them.

Now at the bottom of my apartment building, I wiggled my way through the last of the human obstacles and entered into the safety of the lobby. I quickly found the quiet refuge of the elevator and made my way up to my apartment. I entered the room, my cells still resonating from the energy outside which made the air inside the apartment vibrate. Now that I was in total quiet I could truly appreciate the effect the mob had even on me.

I closed my eyes, took a few deep breaths, and collected myself. My centering was interrupted by Lumi's sweet voice. I opened my eyes to see my angel calmly sitting on one of the chairs in the living room space. Driven by the extra energy from sugary pancakes and celebrating, I rushed to Lumi and we embraced. I held on tight, it was amazing how much I missed Lumi. As I saw more evil and got in the pit with them to erase them, the more I seemed to need Lumi.

After a few kisses and an unbroken ten minute hug, I fell back to Earth and became curious about the visit.

"What are you doing here, Lumi? This is the second time; you are going to bring too much attention to me." I tried to be as sweet and polite as possible, but the viable threat of getting discovered unnerved me.

"Relax Jordan, I got myself assigned to this celebration as well. I argued that being such a large event, involving so many millions of people, more than one scout was necessary." Lumi had been a scout for a lot longer than me and had actually turned down a promotion several times. Lumi's opinions and "recommendations" were taken very seriously.

Lumi knew my mission, but I worried if the reality of it was seen and discovered, the dirty and bloody truth, Lumi might not see me in the same light. Before I could figure out how to voice my concern, Lumi, as if reading my mind, continued.

"I am not here for long. I must be able to report a somewhat different experience from you. But I needed to see you. I will be on my way." Lumi kissed me one last time and disappeared out through my door and into the celebration.

I had to admit I was happy to see Lumi, but I didn't need the distraction. Mr. Michelson had passed me up for another victim, I needed to make sure I was next. I had done everything possible to attract him and I even thought I had him on the hook. Was the blonde just a victim of opportunity? Was I being too difficult or edgy for him? A million questions rushed through my head, none of which I could answer, and many which were now irrelevant.

I changed out of the jersey I had been wearing all night and morning and squeezed myself into something sexier for Mr. Michelson. Once changed, I went to the covered wood table and reviewed what information I had on him, as well as made some notes from what I saw. I worried about if he would need to hunt again this quickly. One way or another I was going to make sure he wanted his hands around my neck. I was going to have to get aggressive and force him to want to take me somewhere secluded.

For the next couple of hours I read and reviewed files on my previous erased targets and those targets I wanted to erase, but never could. I sought some insight into what made Mr. Michelson tick, especially after what I had seen that morning. My mind wandered and betrayed me.

How I wished I could erase the likes of Jack the Ripper, Andrei Chikatilo, Pedro Rodrigues Filho, Pedro Alonso Lopez, Abul Djabar, Hiroshito Ito, D'Andre Johnson, Malik Abdula, Serg Akulov, and many others. But their names were too far engraved in history. My action would be instantly noticed, so I had to take the long tedious path of eliminating the lesser evils and in so doing, try to change the consciousness of a species. No small task, but hell, if I didn't try, who would?

My parents had a sense of humor. Literally, it was programmed into their DNA when they were engineered. When it was their turn to design their child they decided to sprinkle me with comical traits. All children are designed from the limited pool of DNA options. They use the parent's raw material, but quickly modify it to fit the specification. At the end of the design process, a few random and individual attributes are allowed to be chosen for the creature. My parents, in their everlasting search for comedy, choose Curious, Creative, Structured and Unconcerned. Even the neonatal engineer asked them if they were sure. Between giggles and laughs they affirmed their choices.

These few simple traits made me a very odd child, even for an engineered progeny. Many people questioned if I was truly engineered. I fought the Random label hard all my life. It wasn't until Lumi took me as a pupil that I was able to cope with it. I was a very curious person, but cold to most things that would make anyone react. My mind collected a cauldron of random ideas and made sense of it like no one else could. It was that curiosity for the Randoms that had led me here.

I remember clearly the first time I decided to leave San Andreas Island with the pretense of enjoying the North American western beaches. I was young, maybe 17, and my parents really wanted to see me happy before they had to depart. I rode the ferry to North America and as soon as my feet hit solid ground I started heading out into the wilderness. I had heard stories of tribes of Randoms still living in the giant redwood forest. They had been made into child stories to scare children out of the wilderness. Thanks to my parents comedic and tragic choosing of my personality attributes, I was more curious than scared to see what truly lived in the redwood forest.

I had to be stealthy and find a secluded way to leave Civilization. There wasn't a border, not a gate, but frequent drone patrols circulated the boundaries to prevent anyone from leaving or entering Civilization. I chose carefully and made it through undetected. I quickly ran into the overgrown forest in search of my first Randoms. I was curious, but I wasn't foolish. I was armed and ready to defend myself if they tried to make me their next meal.

KIND SAVAGES

I quickly left Civilization behind and worked my way through the forest of giant trees. The anticipation and curiosity kept growing inside of me, while at the same time not letting all the scary stories of the Randoms get to me as I wondered alone through their woods. The giant forest was eerily silent, the only noise coming from the soft ruffle of the leaves above. My feet crunched on the fallen twigs with every step. The knife was tightly gripped inside my right hand. Every distant noise made me turn around and jab at the air in front of me. After the chirping of a bird made me almost cut myself with the sharp blade, I decided I needed to stop and calm my nerves down. I could hear water up ahead and the inviting noise pulled me towards it.

I followed the ever growing sound of the rushing water as I weaved through the giant redwoods. I was amazed at their grandiosity and yet felt somewhat familiar. It finally dawned on me that the perfect building design wasn't anything engineers came upon by computer simulations. The simple honesty of it was that they copied the design of these quiet giants. I looked up at them and the resemblance with the rising cylindrical buildings was all too familiar, except these magnificent trees were alive. While wondering through my internal discoveries, the noise of the rushing water had become louder and I found myself on top of a small hill with a fast moving rocky creek down below.

The water rushed and maneuvered its way through, above and below the maze of smooth boulders and rocks. The wet rocks glistened in what little sunshine the infinite canopies of the redwoods allowed to reach them. The water gurgled and bubbled, foaming and creating miniature eddies. I carefully worked my way down the hill and found a dry, safe boulder to sit on. I watched the water dance and move through the small channels between the boulders and the anxiety I didn't realize I was harboring slowly dissipated.

For the first time since I had been harvested, I was experiencing nature, and I had to admit that it wasn't as scary as the stories told. I allowed my mind to drift and finally set down the knife next to me. As I closed my eyes and studied the aquatic resonances, a voice broke me out of my trance and back into panic.

"What are you doing out here child? You need to get back right this minute!"

My first reaction was to reach for the knife and defend myself. As I fumbled with the knife, it went sliding down the boulder, so did I. I fell from the boulder onto the muddy ground. I made a wet solid sound. I quickly recovered from the tumble and my hands furiously searched through the fallen leaves for my protecting blade. It was nowhere to be found. I heard the voice repeat itself. It was a sweet and very delicate voice, unlike any I had ever heard.

I quickly rose to my feet and prepared my fist for what I expected to be a fight to the death. In front of me stood a woman, I believe, her face looked worn and her hair was a fiery red with sprinkles of white and grey hairs. She was quite stunning, but I had never seen anyone that old, ever. She was fit and her figure quite attractive even for a Random. Her eyes held concern and a little amusement at my impromptu acrobatics.

"Child, what are you doing out here?" I stared at her as if she was speaking a different language, but I understood every word she uttered. She patiently waited for my reply and frown lines formed on her forehead. Mesmerized by the strange sight she was to me, my mouth opened, but not to answer her.

"Ho.. How…. How old are you?" Her amused expression changed to one of confusion and frustration, her blue eyes shooting icy spears at me. She was a genetic anomaly and I had to learn everything about her. Her frown disappeared as she saw my pure and total curiosity about her.

The redhead laughed and her protruding chest bounced as she did. I had learned about mammary glands, but was quite surprised at what they actually looked like. Her eyes held a kindness and she answered my question.

"I am 54, child." She started to walk towards me and I backpedalled until I tripped and my ass met the wet mud once more. She held back her laughter this time, seeing the fear in my eyes.

"Calm down child, I will not hurt you." Her walk slowed and she presented herself as inoffensive as possible. I wanted to get up and run away, but I was petrified by fear and curiosity. How could this woman be 54? My parents were almost 200 and looked younger than her.

As I sat there asking myself a million questions, the redhead made her way over to me. She extended her hand out to help me to my feet. As a reflex I took it and as I was making my way up I was intrigued by the calluses on her palm. Question after question kept storming into my brain preventing me from talking. The kind lady helped me walk over to the hill I had come from and urged me to go back.

"I don't know what you are doing here child, but you must return." Sensing the impending finality of my encounter, I forced my mouth to talk.

"No, no, please... I want... I need... I have so many questions." She kept trying to urge me to leave with her body language, but she finally realized I would not comply. She rolled her eyes and shook her head.

"Fine child, come with me. But just for the night, then you go back." The sun was already heading down and the shadows growing thicker in the giant tree forest. She started to head downstream along the banks of the stream. After a last few moments of hesitation, I followed her.

The stream grew as we walked and eventually the sound of a rushing river could be heard ahead. As I walked I kept feeling tiny little bites all over my exposed skin. Every time I looked at my itching skin I would see small flying bugs suckling on my blood. They would scatter away when I swatted at them, but my skin continued to itch. The redhead noticed my struggle, stopped, and walked back towards me. I had learned about insects, but never experienced their wrath. The feeding sites quickly welted and produced a small red mound on my skin. I was starting to get covered with the small red mounds. The lady finally reached me and pulled a small vial out of her satchel.

"Stand still. I know it itches, but stand still child." She uncorked the small glass vial and poured some of the viscous clear liquid into her other open palm. She started to rub the oily substance all over my exposed skin. Starting with my neck and ears then working her way down my arms. The oily substance smelled of the forest. It was floral, but smelled of pines.

"It is lavender and rosemary; it will keep the bugs away. I am Lucy. What is your name, child?" Lucy kept rubbing the oil on my skin making it slick and shiny. Her eyes held a kindness and concern I had never seen.

"I am Jordan." I wanted to say more, ask her all the questions that were swirling in my mind. Instead, all I could do was stand there, let the kindness in her eyes envelope me, and allow her to tend to me.

"Well, nice to meet you, Jordan." She smiled as she said this, trying to put me at ease. "Why have you wondered out of the civilization, Jordan? Are you running away?" The question caught me off guard since I would have never considered such a thing.

A frown formed on my forehead and I quickly shook my head in disagreement. "No, I would never! I am curious about you..."

"Randoms," she finished for me.

"Yes, Randoms. I have a lot of questions. I am truly amazed how you have even survived." Her kind eyes turned into a disapproving frown.

Realizing my rudeness I tried to explain myself a little better. "I was never scared by the stories. They just made me admire you and want to learn more about you. That is why I am here."

Lucy's expression changed, nodded in approval. She looked up at the sky. "It will be dark soon Jordan, we must get back to the village. We do not want to get caught out in the dark." I sensed her urgency so decided my questions could wait until we were back in her village.

Her speed increased and I kept pace. Thankfully, her oily remedy was keeping the biting bugs at bay. We were now following the large river, but heading upstream this time. The river had carved a channel into the earth and flowed low in the embankment. We walked on top of the bank and I soaked in all the beautiful nature that surrounded us. The plants extended all the way to the river's edge, occupying every single drop of real estate available to them. Larger winged bugs zoomed back and forth showing off the aerial supremacy. Some were skinny rods with four transparent wings. Others were flanked by large colorful wings. The birds would swoop down and catch the slow hovering insects dancing over the water. I had never seen such life and activity and it was spectacular.

I did my best to keep up with Lucy, but found myself several times standing and staring at some new plant, bug, or animal I saw along the fast moving river. Lucy would kindly remind me to move along and I would comply. We eventually reached a well-worn path and followed it away from the river. We were heading back into the giant redwood forest. Along the path a curious tiny river of water followed us along.

The tiny water channel was maybe a meter wide and not much deeper than that. It was lined with rocks and the water gently rippled along it and followed us. I wanted to ask Lucy what it was, but her pace had increased and the distance between us increased. I filed that question with the other 3,591 questions I wanted to ask later. I caught up with Lucy just to get my first glimpse of what must have been her village.

The little channel of water split up in in 3 directions, onwards, to our left, and to our right. We walked over a small stone bridge and were now flanked by rows of tilled soil. Some of the rows lay bare and brown, the rich soil awaiting its new inhabitant. Other rows had tiny sprouts of plants I didn't recognize. Lastly, there were rows with full grown plants which were being tended to by a very elderly couple.

They worked the field to our right which contained the fully grown plants. They smiled and waved at Lucy as soon as they spotted her. They stopped tending to the plants and slowly began to approach us. We kept on the path and eventually we intersected. The grey haired lady quickly gave Lucy a hug. The bald man waited, then gave her his own hug.

"Linda, Mark, this is Jordan." Once the indulgent embraces finished, Lucy introduced me to the elderly couple. Their smiles remained on their faces, but now more muted. The old man extended his right hand towards me. Not knowing what to do, I bowed as it was customary for me. The old lady chuckled and then proceeded to give me a hug. It was an interesting sensation being that close to another person.

"You guys must be hungry; head into the village, supper should be about ready." Linda was still grabbing onto my upper arms and smiling at my naiveté as she said it. Lucy agreed silently with her head and led me further into the village. The couple remained at the path and waved at me every time I looked back at them. I was perplexed at their friendliness and excitement, but resigned myself to wave back every time. I even worked myself up to give them a strained smile.

We kept walking down the worn path and the fields gave way to buildings. They were small, circular, and made out of logs and wood. They echoed the girth of the giant redwoods which provided them shelter, but severely lacked in height. The spaces between the round log homes were decorated with flowers and plants, all of which were exotic to me.

We seemed to be walking towards a larger round building down the path. This one was as wide as the redwoods and I started to hear voices and chatter coming from it. As we walked, I felt something bump into my right leg, and I must have jumped five feet to the left. Once I landed and was done embarrassing myself, two small children ran away from us towards the large circular building. Lucy chuckled at my reaction and kept leading the way.

As we got closer, the voices coming from the building grew in volume and numbers. Through the murmur you could hear laughing and singing. This did not sound like the noises being made by the wild savages of the story. All I had seen so far showed a very friendly and kind people. I knew the stories were exaggerations, but this was beyond my wildest dreams. We finally reached the entrance door to the large round building. Lucy stopped for a second and recognizing the pure panic in my eyes, took a few seconds to calm me down.

"Ok, Jordan. This is our town hall. It is supper time, so everyone is gathered together to share and eat. I am sorry to say that you will stick out like a sore thumb; so just stick next to me and everything will be fine. Oh and please no silly questions, after we eat I will indulge you in your curiosity."

She held me by the shoulders as she spoke and her touch was comforting. I nodded in agreement and she opened the door. Once open the noise grew exponentially and I felt pulled in a hundred directions. Lucy was kind enough to grab me by the hand and lead me through the large hall. Wooden tables with built-in seating lined the hall from my left to my right. After the sea of tables filled with happy Randoms ended, an incredibly long table held all the food for the people.

The lack of structure was overwhelming. People came and went toting full and empty plates of food. Some gathered around the perimeter of the building and engaged in songs or conversations. The kids, the little ones were the worst, buzzing around like hungry bees desperate to find a flower. They bumped into everything, stole food from plates on the tables and people rewarded them by rubbing their heads and laughing at their shenanigans.

"Easy child," Lucy's voice brought me back into my own skin. She was looking down at the vice grip hold I had on her hand. I apologized and loosened my grip on her callused hand. We worked through the madness of the people in the hall until we found our way to the long serving table. The thing had to be at least 20 meters long and every centimeter of it was covered with one type of morsel or another. Lucy handed me a plate and we started to make our way down the table looking for something suitable to eat.

"What do you eat?" Lucy asked me, looking back and forth between me and the serving table. Overwhelmed and confused I shrugged. Once again she rolled her eyes and just grabbed the plate out from my hands. She left me standing as I studied the plates and platters displayed in front of me. There were several kinds of meat. Some displayed as juicy chunks of flesh, others the whole animal. There was a whole roasted pig lying on the table. More than half of it was already missing. I could make out birds of some sort and meats in the shapes of tubes of various colors. Although gruesome looking, the smells were intoxicating. I could feel my mouth water as I caught a whiff of the next hunk of protein.

After the meats, an explosion of color took place on the impossibly long table. Yellows, greens, oranges, and red shone like a rainbow. The smells of the vegetables weren't as mesmerizing, but the colors made you want to grab them and eat them. Lastly, were ten man-sized bowls filled with cooked rice and grains. Being that super was starting to wind down, some of them were empty and the others not very full. Lucy finished filling up my plate and handed it back to me.

I had a few different meats on my plate ranging from white to brown. There were both yellow and orange cylindrical vegetables, the yellow being larger and a nice heaping of white rice. The only thing I was familiar with was the rice; everything else smelled delicious, but could have been a human for all I knew.

We walked over to a table nearby, Lucy slid in first on the bench and I followed her, making sure that I stayed at the end of the table, in case I needed to make a quick exit. I placed my plate down and continued to study it. I hadn't seen any signs that they were cannibals or the monsters of the stories, but maybe they were just happy cannibals. Maybe they were feeding me their last victim and tomorrow it would be me served for supper.

Noticing my hesitation towards the plate full of food, Lucy spoke, "Oh child, relax. The white meat there is chicken, the light brown is the pork you saw on the table, and the dark meat is a blood sausage. The orange are carrots and the yellow corn..." Finally, knowing what she was going to say next, I interrupted and finished for her.

"Rice! That is rice!"

Lucy broke into a full laughter and so did the other people sitting at the table. My overstated excitement truly amused them. "Yes, child, that is rice. Now eat."

I started picking and tasting each delicious morsel on my plate, each one better than the last. Lucy carried on conversation with the people at the table. Most of it was about her adventures with me today. Not knowing what I could say to contribute to the conversation, I just ate. By the time I was done with my plate my stomach felt distended, but I could not stop myself from eating every ounce of food she had served up for me. My tongue had never had the privilege of tasting so much flavor. Lucy somehow finished her plate as well, in between the never ending conversations. She urged me to exit the bench so she could slide out. She grabbed both our plates and led the way. I followed her like a well-trained mascot. Lucy deposited the dull metal plates on top of the stack of other plates and led me out of the town hall.

The village was alive now, people with full stomachs buzzing back and forth enjoying their evening. My nose was still being held hostage by all the smells inside the hall. Even though I was full, both my nose and mouth wanted me to go back and force my stomach to accept more food, even if it hurt. My brain overruled my body parts and I continued to follow Lucy and her crimson flowing hair.

CURIOUS MINDS

We weaved our way through the maze of round smaller buildings. Eventually, she zeroed in on a particular one and we made a bee line towards it. There was a small wooden bench right outside of it, once we approached it she invited me to sit. Once I had sat down, she took the open space next to me on the bench. She turned slightly towards me, placed her hands on the blue skirt that covered her legs, and smiled.

"Go ahead child, ask." Her voice was sweet and inviting. Her face was full of patience and her blue eyes looked as warm as the summer seas. I started and stopped myself several times. I had so many questions and I felt I needed to answer them in the right order. As I sat there mumbling to myself and apparently having a short circuit, she found a way to fill her time. Lucy stood and pulled a small box out of her brown jacket pocket. The small box rattled as she moved it. In front of the grass was a round formation made out of rocks. She went back and forth between the circle made of rocks and a stack nearby with pieces of wood and twigs. She knelt next to the circle of stones and the stack of twigs she had made inside of it. She opened the small box and from inside of it pulled out a small stick of wood with a red black bulbous tip. She struck it against the box and it caught on fire. She carefully reached under the stack of sticks she had arranged and soon the fire had spread from the stick to form a large and dancing flame. She threw a couple of the larger logs on it and found her way next to me on the bench.

"Ok child, you have until that fire burns out. Once it goes out, I am going to bed. I have had a long day and never thought I'd be coming home with a stray. So either ask your questions or we sit here and watch the flames dance and then I go to bed." Her face still held that compassionate look, but her eyes were starting to show how tired she was.

I felt pity for the poor Random woman, so I decided to stop trying to be perfect and just ask the first question that rolled off my tongue. "Are you cannibals and are you planning to eat me?" Not precisely what I thought would come out of my mouth, but fear can make us do some pretty stupid things.

Lucy sat there for a second and then broke out into gut-busting laughter. She bent over herself and slapped her leg as she continued to laugh. Tears started to form on the edge of her eyes and her deep laugh left her gasping for air. She noticed the bewilderment in my eyes and composed herself.

"What have they been telling you kids? You know, never mind. No, we are not cannibals and we are definitely not going to eat you. I mean you are all skin and bones anyways." She winked and poked at my ribs as she said the last part. "Anything else you would like to know?" Her voice still held an edge of laughter and amusement in it.

A little offended by her reaction, I decided to make my next question matter. "Why do you Randoms choose this way of life?"

"Ah... that is more like it." She ignored the contempt in my voice as I said Randoms and contemplated her answer for a second, "We don't choose this "way of life" as you say. This is the natural way of life for us humans. This is how we lived and survived for hundreds of thousands of years and we believe this is the right way to live."

"But look at you, you age prematurely, you must die prematurely as well. And with all the advancement in technology you choose to live in a wooden house and eat dead animals and odd vegetables." I didn't quite ask her a question, but made a counterargument to their lifestyle.

Lucy smiled and continued. "Delicious dead animals, I saw you enjoying every last ounce of them. We don't choose this lifestyle, evolution put us on this course. You are right we age and die, but that is the natural cycle of life. What Civilization has done to life is not right. I think it is pretty safe to say that you have lived more in the last 10 hours than you had the rest of your life. Yes we die, but we also live, oh how we live."

The way she said it, as much as what she said, truly made me wonder. There was a joy and happiness in how she emoted her words and I had to admit it was like nothing I had ever seen before. I wanted to argue with her, we had figured out how to truly evolve as a species, but something in my full gut told me it would have been fruitless, so I moved on to another one of my million questions.

"How do you procreate?" It was a true curiosity of mine and the tall tales and theories I had heard growing up were as numerous as they were preposterous.

Lucy's face became serious and she nodded in agreement with my curiosity. She proceeded to explain to me sex, pregnancy, labor, and childbirth. It was completely alien to me and it sounded more grotesque and fantastic than any of the stories I had heard. I wanted to ask more about it, but overwhelmed with the vivid visual Lucy had provided me, I moved on to my next question.

We spent the rest of the night between questions and confusing answers. She kept listening and answering me way past when the fire died out and when she could no longer help herself but to yawn over and over from exhaustion. She invited me into her round structure and guided me to an extra room. The inside of the structure was as nature filled as the outside. All the furniture was made of wood and plants and herbs decorated and littered the spaces. In the middle of the structure was a metal wooden stove, with a pipe that extended all the way through the roof. We walked past it and my hand gently caressed the cold metal. She opened the door to the room and invited me to enter.

"This was my son's room. He is gone now, so you are welcome to use it." Noticing the new questions in my face she interrupted me. "No, no, no child, enough questions for one night. We can talk about him tomorrow. Tonight you climb into that bed and get some rest. I will get you in the morning so we can make it to breakfast. Good night and welcome to my home." She closed the door and left me alone to wander in the room.

The room was simply decorated just like the rest of the house, and really the whole village. The bed was small, but large enough to accommodate a single human. There was a desk on the far side of the room again made out of wood. There were a couple of plants and a single chair. I grabbed the chair and pulled it up to the desk. I sat on it and tried to imagine what it would have been like to be a Random child and what he must have done at this desk. I opened the drawers and every single one of them was empty, but one. The top left drawer held a single piece of paper. I gently grabbed it, worried it would fall apart in my hands. Its texture was unlike anything I had felt before. There was no need for paper back in Civilization. It was the most unique thing. It looked smooth and at first it felt smooth, but as I rubbed the folded piece of paper between my fingers, I could feel its roughness and its fibers. My delicate fingers could feel every fiber gently interwoven in an infinity matrix, just to create this single piece of paper.

I gently opened it, but now knew that the matrix would hold together and I would not destroy the piece of paper. Once unfolded, I could see that it was some sort of letter. It was written in English so I did the only thing I could, I read it.

Dear Mom,

My time has come and although I know you are frightened and worried about me, I am excited to start on my new journey. I have decided to choose to go north and then join the village on Lake Umatilla. I have heard the fishing is great up there and the girls are not bad either. It will take us five days to get there and I cannot wait. Thank you for everything you have done for me, I promise to make you proud and bring honor to our family name. I will miss you.

I love you with all my heart,
Your son,
Michael

I closed the note and gently placed it back where I had found it. I stood up and numbly put the chair back against the wall. I pulled down the covers on the small bed and gently laid down, my head resting on the pillow. I wasn't tired nor did I need sleep yet, but the letter made something inside of me weak. I was sad for Lucy and her son, although it did sound like he was going to be ok. He definitely should be with a mom like Lucy. What truly made me sad is that it reminded me that in a little less than a year I would be receiving a very similar letter. My letter was going to be from my parents and I was never going to see them again. They would have to submit to the recycling process and like Lucy, I would be left all alone.

I stared upwards towards the ceiling, but was truly looking into oblivion. Today had held such excitement and so many of my questions had been answered. Unfortunately, so many more remained and I didn't know how long I could stay before my parents grew concerned and sent them tracking for me. I wondered if Michael ever made it and what his life must be like up north. I wonder how my life would be once I was indoctrinated into my scout position. I lay in bed wondering and thinking and before I knew it, was wondering through my dreams.

Lucy was gently shaking me and calling out my name. "Jordan, Jordan, time to wake up child." Once I realized morning had come, I sprung out of bed and demanded to know how long I had been sleeping. Lucy informed me that I had to have been out for at least six or eight hours. I knew I was still developing and growing, but four hours should have been my max. I was furious at the situation and found resolve on having had a very busy and different previous day. It didn't matter now, nothing I could do about it. I got ready and followed Lucy once more to the town hall.

The air held moisture and a clean smell. Morning had come and with it a delicate dew which seemed to be covering everything. The air was dense and refreshing as we weaved our way through the homes once more. People seemed to be up and about, all of them happily greeting each other with the fact that it was morning once more. I smiled and nodded when the strangers greeted me and closed the distance between me and Lucy. People were heading in many directions, but the main flow of traffic was towards the town hall. Everyone was awake and everyone was hungry. As we approached the town hall my nose once more was sent into overdrive as my mouth begun to uncontrollably salivate. I didn't know what I smelled, but I wanted to taste it and fill my stomach to my contentment. We entered the hall and as the previous night it was buzzing with excitement.

Instead of shyly following Lucy towards the long table, I hastily made my way towards it. The smells intensified as I approached it, the air was filled with thick rich smells which somehow my brain translated into comforting. Leaving Lucy behind, I made my way to the plates and grabbed one of the dull metal orbs. Again the first things to welcome me were the meats. They smelled heavy and rich and I wanted to try every single one of them.

There were whole legs of pigs sliced pink and vibrant, a variety of tubular shaped meats and ribbons of delectable looking meat. I grabbed some of each and kept working my way down the table. There were trays filled with what appeared to be yellow clouds. I scooped some on my plate and continued. The breads were plentiful and I grabbed a few different shaped and colored ones. Lastly, I reached what I thought were vegetables, but later discovered were oh so different and so much more delicious. My plate was overflowing, so I had to resort to tucking some of the sweet vegetables under my arm as I found my way to a table.

Once I sat down a kind woman came by, set down a dull metal cup with a handle and filled it with a dark and mysterious liquid. She asked if I wanted sugar and cream. Unsure of what to say, I smiled and nodded once more. She then produced a small serving cup and spilled some white dense liquid into the cup as well as put in two spoonful of a white powder and mixed it with a stick for me. She asked me if that was ok, I nodded yes and she went on her way with her tray filled with mysterious liquids and powders.

I dove into my plate with the gusto of a starving man. The saltiness, the sweetness, the creaminess of it all was mind altering. Every new bite was a wonderful and cataclysmic experience. I filled my mouth until I could almost not swallow. I grabbed the elixir the nice lady poured in my metal cup and discovered an even more delicious treat. It was sweet, creamy, a little bitter, acidic, and savory, it truly grabbed every single taste bud in my mouth by the neck and slapped their individual faces. After I took my sip, I stared into the cup as if I was going to be able to find heaven inside of it.

Lucy sat across from me and smiled at my amazed and enchanted expression. "It is called coffee, child. I see you are hungry, nice heaping plate you got yourself there." Coffee, it was called coffee and it tasted of immortal and blissful life.

In between bites I was able to ask Lucy a few questions. "Why did your son leave? If I may ask, Lucy."

She smiled and her face filled with pride. It was not the reaction I was expecting. Once she started explaining, her expression made more than sense.

"Michael left to go up North and seek a new village. He was one of the best hunters in this village and well sought after by all the surrounding villages. He turned eighteen and as it is customary in our way of life, all the males leave their village at that age and move to a different one." Either the look of bewilderment painted on my face or the fact that I had asked poor Lucy so many questions made her explain more before I could ask. "It is about genetic diversity and keeping the species in touch with itself. We trade genes, traditions, and information this way. You see those boys in that table over there?" She pointed her worn hands over to her right. "Those boys arrived from many villages. Some of them, like my Michael, were the best suitors from their villages. They will join us; help us and each find themselves a wife. This is a very special time for us all over the land."

She finished talking, but the smile lingered on her face, as her eyes wondered into another place. She was filled with pride, where I was filled with dread at the upcoming recycling of my parents. I nodded, letting her know I understood and kept my fears to myself. She kept smiling as she went back to her plate full of food.

I spent the next three nights learning many a thing about the Randoms and I must admit I became quite enamored with their way of life. It was the way history books described previous civilizations and somehow they made it work. The Randoms were being friendly and hospitable to me, but who knew for what purposes. They fed me, Lucy hosted me, and they never tried to eat me. As I had suspected they were not the savages they were painted out to be.

Many more questions about why the Randoms had gained such a violent and hostile reputation rushed through my head. Had it all been lies made by Civilization? And if so, why? I would have to find the answer to those questions on my own; there really wasn't anyone I could ask either here or back home.

Everyone in the village made me feel welcome and I got to know a few of the people. Lucy had taken me under her wing and that was good enough for them. That all changed on the fourth morning.

Lucy and I were strolling through the maze of round houses making our way to the town hall. It was morning time and the dew was covering everything. The grass looked more green and vibrant, being a little wet. There were invisible birds chirping and making happy sounds as they woke up themselves. The dirt on the path cracked under my shoes as we walked. Lucy, becoming used to my company, was the happiest I had seen her since she found me on the river. The morning was brisk, but not quite cold. The cool air was somehow refreshing and invigorating as it caressed my skin and filled my lungs. The redwoods still loomed way above us and provided refuge from any sky bound sentry.

I had asked Lucy and others hundreds of questions and they kindly fulfilled my curiosity each time. The problem was that every answer seemed to lead to more questions. I was peppering Lucy with questions as we walked. She would listen and answer, her smile never breaking her face. We were almost to the town hall when I felt a small splatter on the right side of my face. I looked up expecting to see droplets falling down on me from a redwood. If they had fallen from them it would have been impossible to tell. The giant trees extended upward so far that their canopies were just a blur of green. I rubbed my hand against the wet spot on my face, only to find my fingers stained with crimson.

I looked to my right just to see Lucy's body start to fold on itself and fall to the ground. She lay on the ground eyes open with a small red dot on her forehead. The dot was slowly oozing thick and red liquid out of her forehead. The screams began to fill the tranquil morning air and the village buzzed like an angry beehive. People young and old scrambled and ran throughout trying to escape their unnamed hunters.

My first thought was a rival tribe. Maybe I was about to witness and experience the true savage nature of the Randoms. I looked around and scrambled trying to find shelter. Unfortunately, my feet refused to cooperate and I stood there as easy frozen prey as it all unfolded. Everything began to slow down; the people running were now walking in exaggerated motions. All of the noises disappeared and my eyes were seeing in extreme detail. I looked down at Lucy, her eyes open and empty, still looking back at me. The small hole on her forehead had now let enough blood free as in to cover most of the top of her head. Her beautiful red hair now had a very different and much more sinister shade. I looked up just in time to see a small child, being pulled along by his mom, find the same fate as Lucy. A crimson spot appeared on their foreheads, their eyes went blank, and their bodies hit the ground mid-stride. The path released a small cloud of dust welcoming the bodies into its hard and unforgiving buxom.

Random after Random crisscrossed the paths as I stood there petrified. Each one of them sprouting a red dot on their foreheads and hitting the ground violently. Pretty soon the wet grass was now being soaked in red blood. The bodies littered the ground, old, young, and even infant. All of them lay motionless on the ground and I could have sworn I heard the redwoods cry. I started to hear footsteps and they all seemed to be converging on me. As the camouflaged figures moved through the bodies they made sure every single one of them was truly dead. They would stop at still moving ones and dispense a few more shots from the weapons they were brandishing. As they came closer to me, I worried about which tribe they belonged to, and why they would do such an atrocious thing. I stood there as the leader made its way to me. The fully camouflaged figure, once in front of me, removed its mask and addressed me.

The face staring back at me surprised me, paralyzing my mouth to match my unmoving feet. I expected a savage, a monster, an angry Random, instead in front of me stood a beautifully engineered face, symmetrical to a fault, beautiful and gentle. The eyes in it were serious and focused. Its succulent lips moved, and after the third or fourth time, I was able to hear what it was trying to say to me.

"Are you Jordan?!" The beautiful figure kept scanning the grounds for any possible threats. I did all I could and mumbled out a yes. The beautiful camouflaged figure continued. "Your parents are waiting for you; people were worried you were dead. You are safe now, we are taking you home."

In front of me stood one of mine, not a Random, a monster, or some deranged villager. Instead, my people had slaughtered everyone for the sake of finding me. I stood there and pondered who the savages and monsters really were.

I was grabbed by the wrist and led through a now budding inferno. The homes and buildings were set ablaze as we were careful not to trip over the bodies. My feet made splashing sounds as I was running through the blood soaked grass. I was pulled along by the leader and escorted by a small squadron of soldiers. The heat coming from behind me made me look; the welcoming and happy village was now engulfed in dancing flames. Most disturbing was how the bodies, not being able to escape the flames, joined in the fiery dance. Everything and everyone burned, the sizzling and popping sounds along with the strange smells of burning wood and flesh, overwhelmed my brain. I had to stop. I had to do something. I pried my wrist out of the soldiers grip and started running back toward the burning city. I knew I could not save anyone, they were already dead. But there had to be something I could do. I ran, my mind blank and my feet leading the way. The heat was becoming overwhelming and before I knew it I stood in front of Lucy's house.

Flames were dancing on the roof just like her fiery red hair danced on her head. I kicked in the door, took a deep breath, and plunged into the flames. The house was full of smoke and the now open door started to feed the fire inside. I rushed through the house and to my final destination. I walked into Michael's room and it was still safe from the flames. I opened the desk drawer and found Michael's letter to his mother. I fetched it and hid it in my inside coat pocket. I turned to exit the room just in time to find the welcoming living space turned into a fire filled pit. I placed both hands over the letter, safely kept inside my coat, and darted through the fire as fast as I could.

I exited the now collapsing house coughing and gasping for air. Some of the hair on my body felt singed, but it was all worth it. I had saved Lucy, at least part of her. Outside, the squadron met me and made sure I was alright. They led me once more out of the flaming village, through the woods, and back to Civilization. Numb and a little dead inside, I didn't fight or resist them this time. I let them whisk me away and return me back to my parents.

My parents welcomed me with as much emotion as they could and cared for me for the next few days. I spent most of that time resting alone in my room and reading Michael's letter. I read it over and over and over again until I knew every curve and line of his writing; until I could recite it with my eyes closed. Every time I would see Lucy's proud face as she spoke of Michael. I would see her smile and the kindness she had shown me. I could imagine her reading the letter when she first found it. I read and forced myself to remember every detail about Lucy and the village; until the letter read itself to me in her voice and until I made sure I would never forget her.

I found myself holding a paper and caressing it like I caressed the letter every time I read it. It was a random piece of paper, until I snapped out of my trance and saw what was truly on it. It was a summary of a medieval serial killer called Vlad the 3rd. Most serial killers are damaged by life and become monsters. A few through history actually were just born and wired that way. Vlad the 3rd had done atrocious things for the shock value of it, showing no remorse for it. I kept looking for what made Mr. Michelson tick, I believed I had found it. He was a psychopath, there had to be no rhyme or reason for his actions, they just were. He enjoyed it and felt as much guilt for killing those girls as he felt swatting a fly. He was never diagnosed and it never came up during his case or accounts, but I was certain now of what he really was. Know your prey so you can properly hunt it.

I spent the rest of the night making my plan on how to coax Mr. Michelson the next day. I wasn't in a rush yet, but the sooner I could button this up, the better. As I did every night, before my slumber, I pulled out Michael's letter. The paper was now soft from so much handling and creased from being hidden folded in its envelope. I pulled out the letter more for the feel than for the words. I rubbed the old piece of paper between my fingers as I closed my eyes and saw Lucy in my mind's eye. I heard her recite every word in the letter with pride on her face. Lucy's face dissipated, I put the letter safely once more next to my body and went to sleep.

DAY 2

I woke up determined to end this cat and mouse game today. Whether Mr. Michelson wanted to accept it or not, today I was going to erase him from the ethos. I knew I could not trigger him like other killers; all I could do was present myself as a possible victim and let his mind act on it. I would make sure he saw enough of me today so he would want to get rid of me. I went to the mostly empty closet and grabbed my Cubs regalia out from it. I put my long hair in a ponytail and went out to search for Mr. Michelson.

I decided his apartment should be my first target. He lived close to his work in a swanky downtown apartment. I made short work of the walk. The cool morning lake breeze reminded me of my walk with Lucy that morning. With every authoritative step I took down the hard pavement, I distanced myself from the memory. The building stood tall in front of me, still in its antiquated square form. It reached high into the sky and somewhere in there Mr. Michelson was probably shaving, getting ready for his dual life day. I wanted him to really notice and target me, not try to avoid my smothering. It was a fine balance, so I decided to find shelter from the cold morning breeze in the coffee shop on the lower level of the building.

I entered through the glass door and was received by a very eclectic crowd. Inside, a mix of suits and Cubs jerseys speckled the crowd with greys, blacks, white, and blues. It was day two of the celebration, according to records it almost ended this day. Instead, the crowd was just getting their second wind and the celebration would continue until the parade on the fourth day.

I got in line to kill time and wait until a table near the windows became open. The line was slow and the patrons impatient. They needed their drug and they needed it now. The girl behind the counter took orders as

51

fast as possible and took the needy patrons money. Two other girls along with a young man scurried around behind the oversized and shiny machines putting together all the capricious concoctions that had been ordered. Steam plumed and devilish noises came out of the machines as they kept moving in the intense dance. Cups would appear on another counter along with the shout of names as they were placed down by one of the frantic girls. When the impatient patrons would hear their name they would almost run up to the counter, grab their bounty, and go to another station to doctor it to their liking. Everyone made the same expression as they took their first sip out of the hot cups. First their face scrunched trying to block out the ungodly temperature of the liquid, then bliss. Their bodies would relax and a tension they didn't realize they were harboring disappeared. Their shoulders relaxed, the grip on the cup eased and some of them even shivered as if having an orgasm.

I moved along in the line watching this show of desperation and relief; repeat itself over and over again, until it was my turn to order. I ordered a macchiato, threw a $100 on the counter, and walked away from the overworked girl. I stood along the front wall of glass windows making sure Mr. Michelson hadn't snuck past me, and waited for the other girl to scream my name and make my cup appear on the counter.

The quiet streets were starting to buzz once more. Hangovers dissipating and coffee kicking in, the celebration was starting to come in like the rising tide. "Jordan!" I looked back just to see the white cup resting alone on the brown counter. I grabbed it and found a stool along the window so I could wait for Mr. Michelson to rise and join the festive streets.

I sipped on the hot elixir & took mental notes of the crowd outside for my official report. Eventually, Mr. Michelson's figure crossed in front of me outside the glass. He was strolling slowly arm in arm with a tall, and beautiful woman. She was almost as tall as him, wearing a sexy, but out of place cocktail dress and had her brown hair in a ponytail to hide the mess they made of it the previous night. Her white teeth refused to hide and she could not stop smiling and giggling as he kept talking to her. She forced the teeth back just to give him a kiss, she turned, he gave her a loving spank and she was on her way, smiling and with a spring to her step.

Why he killed some and not others was starting to frustrate me. How did I make myself be one of the ones he wanted and needed to kill? I shook the doubt in my mind and reminded myself I could not be outsmarted by such a primitive human. I abandoned my stool, went out to the streets, and followed Mr. Michelson from a safe distance. He was certainly heading to work and I could not let him spend all day away from me. I caught up to him and made sure to bump into him as I passed him. I apologized for my rudeness and his eyes lit up with recognition. I kept walking and let him make his move. Even if not hungry, a predator cannot resist the urge to hunt.

"Jooo…. Jordan right?!" I looked back and pretended to not recognize him. I gave him a puzzled look to further trigger his hunting reflex. "Yes, Jordan from The Sea Urchin. What are you doing in this part of town, darling? Oh and how rude of me, good morning." After he wished me a good morning he gave me his best and most seductive smile. He was a handsome man, but that was irrelevant to me. I forced myself to play the swooned girl and started to walk back towards him.

"Yes, I am Jordan, you must forgive me, but I forgot your name." He stood there content as he reeled his catch in with just his smile. Once I was close enough for his comfort, he reminded me of his name. "Pat," he said his name and I could swear he purred as he said it like some sort of feral cat. His hand instantly reached out and grabbed me by the small of my back and before I knew it I was being hugged. I hugged him back, amazed at how truly smooth he was.

"I must say Jordan, you are even more beautiful in daylight. May I buy you breakfast?" I fought back a gag at this regurgitated line, but accepted. I needed him close. We walked down the sidewalk until we reached a bakery shop. He opened the door for me and led me in. We ordered some sweet delicious treats and sat down at a small table. He unbuttoned his charcoal suit jacket and sat across from me. His eyes fixated on mine, while giving me a slight smile.

I sat there and pretended to be shy. Smiling back and making only momentary eye contact. I dove in to the small plate before me and did some culinary research. Instead of coffee, I decided to try the hot chocolate along with my pastry. Just like the girl behind the counter implied, it was heavenly.

"Ever been here before, Jordan?" His tone was perfect, seductive but still playful. His words rode the edge of creepy and sexy. I could see why his victims would go along with anything he said.

"Nope, first time and it is delicious. How about you? Come here often alone?" He could not hold back the quick laugh that escaped his chest. He composed himself and I continued. "Not that I care, just curious, chocolate and pastries are the way to a girls heart."

"Let's just say I have been here various times, some alone and some not. I see you are still celebrating the Cubs Championship." He nodded towards the jersey.

"I see you are not." I raised my eyebrows and looked at his boring, but stylish charcoal suit.

"The world doesn't get to stop for all of us. My clients expect me to represent them and take very good care of them, so I do."

I played naïve to keep the conversation going. "Clients?"

"Yes, clients." I gave him an inquisitive look, urging him to continue. After a couple of seconds, he could not resist bragging about himself, so he continued. "I am a corporate lawyer, let's say some of my clients are very influential in the city and have a lot of very important projects I need to oversee. They take very good care of me, so I make sure their plans don't hit any snags."

The arrogance and pride oozing out of him made my hot chocolate taste bitter as I sipped on it. He was a good looking man, had money and strode the line of confidence and douchebag pretty narrowly. If I didn't erase him, the ripples could be even bigger than what I had given him credit for.

I smiled and we continued with the small talk until our plates and cups were empty. After establishing himself as someone desirable, he peppered me with question after question. I had never been so glad I made myself a very good and solid identity. Usually the targets want to get me alone right away making erasing them a lot quicker and easier. Mr. Michelson on the other hand was seriously trying to get to know me.

He walked me out once more opening doors and being the perfect gentleman as we exited the bakery. We stood facing each other on the sidewalk as the celebration was once more in full swing around us. He grabbed my hands, thanked me for an enjoyable breakfast, and gave me a gentle kiss on the lips. He handed me his fancy business card, told me to call him, then turned away and was on his way. I had to give him credit, he was smooth. It was that smoothness and arrogance which lead too many other half handsome businessmen to think they could get away with anything. Many women were raped and murdered and he was the rock that started that ripple in the business world. I will erase him no matter how charming he might think he is.

Mr. Michelson was heading into work, it would have been futile to follow him there just so I can sit in the lobby and wait again. I decided that since Lumi was along for the experience this time, we might as well celebrate together. I opened my wrist control and set my tracker to find Lumi. I strolled through the celebrating crowd, breakfast beers were being passed around and the Go Cubs Go game was starting to echo through the streets. It was a happy and jubilant crowd. I could not help myself from smiling and giving out high fives as they were requested. After twenty or so blocks I finally spotted my Lumi. Lumi was indulging with a beer in each hand, while swaying back and forth and singing along with the crowd. Lumi hadn't spotted me yet so I carefully weaved my way through the crowd as to remain undetected. I was enjoying seeing Lumi like this, celebrating and not having to be the elder responsible Scout.

Lumi was wearing a Cubs pinstriped jersey and blending in better than I could ever dream of. If I didn't know who Lumi was, I would have not thought twice about it. I went around trying to surprise Lumi from the back. I made sure not to be seen and moved very slowly as I approached Lumi. As always, a couple of seconds before I could claim my unsuspecting victim, Lumi called out my name. "Hi Jordan, nice try." Never failed, I accepted my defeat with a smile and hugged my Lumi from behind. I have been trying for years, never once successfully startling or even scaring Lumi.

"Are you ever going to give up? You are never going to get me." Lumi smiled and hugged me back, as well as someone can hug someone else with their back, and handed me one of the beers. I joined the celebration and signing, and lost myself with Lumi for the rest of the day.

We drank, bar hopped, met a lot of friendly people and worked our way through the celebrating city. Before I knew it, the sun was starting to set, which meant Mr. Michelson would be reentering the streets soon. I wanted to make sure to have eyes on him as soon as he did. I told Lumi I had to leave and left before I could change my mind. Today had been one of the most fun days I ever spent with Lumi. I had never seen Lumi so loose and relaxed and it pulled me in even more.

We drank together, that was a first. I knew Lumi had drunk before; we had discussed it when talking about our missions. I had just never witnessed it with my own two eyes. Lumi embraced the spirit of what the alcohol should do to a person and became the friendliest and happiest "non-drunk" I had ever seen. We made out in public and Lumi groped me in ways I didn't know a human could be touched. We danced, we sang, it was the closest I had ever felt like a human. It was the closest I felt like I had a real human partner. I even saw a gleam in Lumi's eye I had never seen before, maybe I saw it or maybe I imagined it. Either way I left before I could really dwell on the magnificent day I had.

I left the bar where we had been celebrating and started my walk back towards Mr. Michelson's office building. My plan was to tail him for a bit, then run into him by accident. Hopefully, that would prompt a dinner invitation and a murder attempt. I could only hope, I wanted this done and didn't want another poor girl to suffer the same fate as yesterday's blonde.

I walked with a purpose, my smile was replaced with a determined look, and I even got heckled for refusing to give high fives as I walked. I needed to make it to Mr. Michelson's building and time was not on my side right now. The streetlights began their blooming illumination, slowly becoming more brilliant as the sun exited the sky's stage. I picked up the pace as I started getting closer, only to bump into one of the few not happy drunks strolling the streets.

"What's your problem, dude?!" The man somehow mumbled while swaying back and forth, while pointing at me with a beer wielding hand.

"I said, what is your problem, buddy? You think you're so cool with your pony tail don't you?" I stared and studied the belligerent drunk and pondered my options. He was a tall man with a scruffy long beard and expensive watch. He sported a cut off jersey with tattoo covered arms sprouting out of it. He threw his half empty can of beer towards my feet and it splattered all over my boots. Someone had definitely pissed in his cereal and he was going to make me his outlet.

The large man stepped towards me and the chain that connected his ripped blue jeans and wallet jingled as he walked. As he got closer, he began to tower over me until I was face to face with his long brown beard. He smelled of beer and puke as he swayed back and forth while poking me in the chest with his pointer finger. The left pointer finger like him was fat and oversized and he intended to intimidate me with it. His glassy eyes kept trying to stare at me and give me a dirty look, but it was obvious he didn't know which "me" to look at through his drunken stupor.

He kept mumbling and spitting words in my direction as his eyes continued to fill with rage. I saw his right muscular arm pull back and prepare to strike me. His movement slowed and even the mild mist that was falling from the grey clouds became suspended in the air. His mouth began to move slowly and I could appreciate how little care he had paid to his teeth. His fist formed and slowly started to move in the direction of my face. I truly didn't have time to waste, but I didn't want to blow my cover either. I watched the meaty fist move through the air, small droplets of rain gently splashing on it.

As I decided how to handle my new oversized drunk friend, I moved out of the way of his right fist. He missed and I watched as he slowly pulled back his left for a follow up. I looked around to see whose attention our little argument had captured. Luckily, only one person was watching the fight unfold. It must have been his friend because they were both dressed to match and had signed the same no shave pact. He was holding a beer and slowly swaying back and forth under the prettified mist. It was obvious he was extremely drunk as well, so I felt pretty safe on making quick work of the situation.

His new friend's left arm was still cocking back. Even if I wasn't seeing everything in slow motion, this poor guy really liked to telegraph his punches. I swung my right hand palm open and struck the side of the neck of my bearded friend. I made sure to strike hard enough to put him to sleep, but not hard enough to kill him. For good measure, I pulled down his pants around his ankles. I released my pony tail, letting my hair loose, turned and walked away. As time sped up for me once more, the large man crumpled to the ground and his friend was left looking mesmerized. I kept walking and didn't look back and all I could hear as I increased the distance between us was his friend trying to help his fallen comrade. "What the hell Donny, you ok?"

I couldn't help chuckling, but was a little annoyed at the large man.

Hopefully, he didn't make me miss Mr. Michelson, otherwise I might have to come back and really pull a number on him.

EASY PREY

The moon was full and shone through the low misty and grey clouds. The wind picked up and paid full homage to the city's nickname. People started to seek shelter from the cold night, but many remained outside celebrating, warmed by the spirits running through their veins. I made the last corner and realized I might have to pay the large bearded man a visit later. Mr. Michelson had left work and was walking arm in arm with a sexy little number of a woman.

She was sexy, yet sophisticated. She wore a short grey skirt with a white blouse and grey jacket to match. It looked very professional, but not as expensive as his charcoal suit. He kept smiling and looking at her like a lion looks at a gazelle. She kept smiling and twirling her hair like a smitten schoolgirl. I didn't know where he had found her, but he had hooked her and was reeling her in. She was a young gal, early twenties would be my estimation, her hair was brown and her eyes a vibrant blue. They stood on the sidewalk across from me as the mist started to dampen their business clothes.

A strong gust of wind blew and she visibly shivered as the cold air caressed her exposed skin. He took the opportunity and pulled her in closer to him, offering his strong tall body as warmth. She didn't resist and soon their faces were but an inch from each other. He wrapped his arm around her waist and led her down the sidewalk. Hopefully just to dinner and not her untimely death.

I followed close behind from across the street. Making sure to stay close enough to get every detail of their interaction, but not too close as in to be noticed by him; although I think I could have been right behind them and Mr. Michelson would not have noticed. He was as entranced as she was, and his eyes never wavered away from his new companion.

The mist let up, the clouds made themselves sparse, and the full moon shone bright in the night sky. The wind was still howling and swirling around and through the building, but the misting had stopped. It was a perfectly chilly yet romantic autumn's night. Mr. Michelson finally took his prey into what appeared to be an Italian restaurant. I watched from outside as the maître d' quickly recognized Mr. Michelson and whisked the couple back to a booth. Thankfully, I was still able to keep an eye on Mr. Michelson from outside, but the booth only allowed me to see his young female companion.

Everyone in the restaurant was very well dressed so there was no way to sneak in with my Cubs jersey. I couldn't gamble and go change either, by the time I got back I might lose Mr. Michelson. I had no real options so I found a covered stoop and watched the poor girl get reeled in. The waiter came along to their table sporting his penguin tuxedo. The girl started to fumble through the menu, but quickly calmed as the attention of the waiter was completely directed towards Mr. Michelson. I could not see him, but I could see his arms moving in the air as he talked to the attentive server. He was obviously ordering for himself and her. She smiled and made excited expressions at whatever he was ordering for her. The waiter soon left and her eyes were once more fixated on the blind side of the booth.

She kept nervously twirling her hair on and off and his hands would reach across the table to caress her blushing face. The waiter returned with a bottle of wine and went through all the rigmarole with Mr. Michelson of tasting the wine before serving it. The girl watched intently obviously impressed. After all the wine formalities ended, the waiter served two glasses and the girl eagerly reached for it to taste. He quickly stopped her as I saw him elevate his glass for a toast. Whatever he said made her blush so hard it even reached her neck. She made that wiggle that insinuated she was blushing in much more private places. Their wine glasses met and she finally got to taste the red elixir.

The dinner progressed, course after course being brought to the booth, along with multiple bottles of wine. The girl seemed to be enjoying every morsel as well as being more and more impressed by Mr. Michelson. The wine was starting to get to her, her face remained permanently blushed and her eyes ever so slightly more shiny and glassy. She was getting every girls wish of being wined and dined by a rich man at a fancy restaurant. She was his, even if she didn't realize it. Her hands kept searching across the table to hold his and at one point he stood and met her half way over the table for a soft and sensuous kiss.

Once dessert had been served and fed to her by Mr. Michelson, she left the table probably to go to the ladies room. He sat there and the only thing I could see was his left hand. His finger rhythmically tapped the table, starting with his pinky and gracefully moving towards his pointer finger. His hand moved with a calmness and anticipation. He knew he had her, now it was just a matter of deciding what he wanted to do with her. Have his way with her or kill her.

She came back from the bathroom looking a little more radiant for him. He threw some money on the table and then exited the restaurant into the chilly night. She instantly cuddled in to the pit of his arm and he willingly embraced her. They walked snuggled into each other as he was starting to pave the way towards the lake. She didn't know where he was leading her, but I could tell that the lake was his destination once more.

I thought of the blonde still probably floating just under the surface of the lake. Slowly decomposing and becoming part of the food chain. I needed to figure out how to stop him tonight without blowing my chances of erasing him organically. I didn't want to just erase the fear that fed into the consciousness of civilization. It also needed to happen in a fashion where victims were empowered and fear squashed. That is why I needed to be his victim and why I could not just take him out at will.

Night had come and the streets were now in full celebratory mode. Tomorrow was the parade; people were either preparing for it or celebrating for it. The city had waited a long, long time for this to happen and everyone was going to experience as much celebration as possible.

I considered intercepting them and either giving him a "drunk" kiss or pretending to be someone to him to scare the girl away. Either way, I would have blown my chances with him later. I was good at becoming invisible while following Mr. Michelson, but now I needed to get close enough to blow my cover. I had already seen him strangle the life out of one girl; I was not in the mood to witness it again.

I made my move to close the distance between us. I had to stop my advances as he pulled her into the stoop of a building. It was dark, but I could clearly see them. They were passionately kissing while their hands searched hungrily over each other's bodies. His hands found the end of her knee high business skirt and started to explore upwards. She gasped at his touch on her thighs. Her head tilted back and her knees slightly bent as he found more intimate places under her skirt. He kissed her neck as she left it exposed as she was taken away to another place.

I hung back and watched. Maybe he had changed his mind, maybe it was too cold and too dark for him tonight. Maybe he would play with her a bit and then let her go. Thankfully, the girl robbed him of any decision he might still be debating. Her body stiffened and her eyes were filled with an irritated annoyance. She stopped him as she furiously searched inside her purse. She pulled out the lit apparatus, pressed a button, and put it to her ear. She listened and answered with short snappy replies. She hung up and clenched her jaw as she shook her head from side to side. She stomped her left foot down and clenched her fist as she did. Mr. Michelson was no longer exploring her neck with his mouth and gave her room to vent. She apologized over and over to him, gave him one last kiss, and left him standing in the dark stoop by himself. Her heels forcefully stomped on the ground as she walked away, once more exploring her phone as she walked.

He stood there for a while gathering himself. He was polite and understanding as she apologized, but I could almost see the heat exiting his body right now. He looked around and for a second I worried that he had spotted me. I had gotten a little careless when approaching them to stop him and now I was left a little exposed. He stared right in my direction, I did my best to stand still, and become invisible. He looked in the shadow of the stoop I hid in for a longer time that was comfortable. Eventually he snapped out of his searching trance, gave a look to each side, and reentered the sidewalk. He headed back into the heart of the city. I stood there and waited, giving him plenty of time and distance before I exited the darkness of my almost blown hiding spot.

By the time I figured it was safe and started my search for Mr. Michelson, I had lost him in the growing crowd. I was so worried about saving that poor girl that I might have actually lost him for the night. The streets were once more filled with chants and hollering from the ecstatic city dwellers. You couldn't help but to smile at their pure joy. I kept exchanging smiles and frowns as I weaved my way through the crowd. To my disappointment, Mr. Michelson was nowhere in sight. I was powerless to track him down or find him. He might have gone home or he might have found another victim. Either way, I could do nothing about it. I accepted my temporary defeat and decided to go back to The Sea Urchin. That made me smile; Mike was starting to grow on me.

I set my bearing and slowly advanced my way through the busy sidewalk and streets. I finally turned the corner and a familiar and confusing sign called out to me. The streets were even fuller down here. People were bar hopping and The Sea Urchin was benefitting from the festivities. I walked into the sticky bar and Mike nodded and welcomed me in his own unique fashion. He was buried behind a wake of demanding patrons at the bar. His attention was quickly back on them, as he handed beers and drinks into their hungry hands.

I scanned the place hoping to find Mr. Michelson there by chance, but was quickly disappointed. I worked my way to the only open table left and proceeded to scan and study the unusually full bar.

The bar was a wall of jerseys and t-shirts, all of them sporting an eclectic mix of numbers and names. Here and there were the after work shirts breaking up the sea of numbers. It was the first night I had seen every table filled. Groups and couples huddled in them drinking, talking, and smiling. The usual dark and sad bar was filled with smiling faces and joy. It seemed wrong, but I guess even the most depressed soul can smile when the seemingly impossible happens.

I kept my eye on the door hoping Mr. Michelson's familiar smug face would grace me with his presence. Unfortunately, the flow of unknown happy faces kept pouring in and out of the bar, but Mr. Michelson was nowhere in sight. A waitress delivered my usual Cuba Libre to my table as she pointed back towards the bar. Mike held up two fingers on his right hand in my direction. I lifted the drink and thanked him with a smile and a nod. It was the first time I had seen a waitress in this place and before I could give her a tip, she was off and running, delivering drinks and picking up empty glasses from the tables.

The girl moved with urgency and her big circular tray never seemed to be empty. She wasn't the prettiest thing in the world, but she had a nice smile and was showing off as much cleavage as her black shirt would let her. Below her ample buxom was a big, barrel-chested torso. The femininity kept disappearing as I studied more of her body. Narrow hips, flat ass and skinny legs, the poor girl didn't have much to work with, but she smiled and kept getting her tips. Her black hair was pulled up in a pony tail that danced and moved in the opposite direction she was moving.

She saw me looking at her and our eyes met. It wasn't until then that I realized who she had to be. Her eyes were the same dead blue as Mike's. She smiled at me and the faces were indistinguishable. Mike had a sister, who knew. She was working hard and kept the flow of booze going on the tables and Mike took care of the bar. Businesses like this will probably make more money in these 4 days than they make all year, Mike was wise to call in the reinforcement. She stopped by my table to check in on me.

"Need anything else, baby girl?" Her voice, unlike her, was very sensual and feminine. She smiled and continued to chew her gum as she waited for my answer. I smiled back and asked for another drink. She went on her way to look for my drink. Nights like this I wished I could get drunk. One of the joys of being genetically engineered to resist all toxins, is that you also resist the most basic and most celebrated ones. CH_3-CH_2-OH might be very inoffensive and basic compared to other toxins, but I was still immune to it. I kept drinking the delicious Cuba Libres and Mike's sister kept bringing them to me. I watched the crowd, wished for blurry vision, and the sight of Mr. Michelson's face.

The waves of fans circulated in and out of the bar, taking it from almost empty to bursting at the seams. The cycle repeated itself over and over throughout the night. The rum and cokes kept coming and I kept drinking them. The faces, the jerseys, and the numbers blended into each other and I knew staying was futile. I kept hoping, but Mr. Michelson eluded me for another night. I was bound and determined to make this his last night, but my prey proved more slippery than I thought.

Defeated, I left a few hundred dollar bills on my table and exited the busy bar and out into the cool streets. People were still pounding the pavement celebrating and rejoicing. The vast majority of them did appear to be moving in the same general direction. Still not tired and with nothing better to do, I decided to follow the flow of humanity. It was close to four in the morning. The crowd flowed like a river of bodies and was comprised of the usual drunken, celebrating fans. To my surprise there were also families with children.

The kids walked wide-eyed, holding on to their parents' hands as they soaked in as much as they could of the night. Smaller ones were pushed along in strollers. Big piercing eyes shone out from the strollers as they were unable to sleep with the electricity in the air. The thickness of the flow increased as we moved along, but everyone remained cordial and considerate, especially toward the children.

I could feel the electricity in the air as we finally reached the destination, Michigan Avenue. The masses spilled onto both sides of the street and people jockeyed for real estate. The parade was to start at Harry Caray's Tavern on the pier, go up Michigan Avenue to Clark, and end up at Wrigley Field. Everywhere I looked the streets were already filling with eager fans on both sides. Some had brought chairs and made themselves comfortable. Others stood, drank, and chatted with their neighbors. Others had found a home in the pavement, some of them were even sleeping amongst the safety of the herd. As the sidewalks filled up with fans on both sides it reminded me of ancient armies lining up and preparing for battle. I was pretty certain that there would not be any bloodshed amongst these facing armies.

I found myself helplessly scanning the crowd for Mr. Michelson, but he was still nowhere to be found. In my everlasting search, I did run into a familiar and much more beautiful face, Lumi. Lumi had already found a front row spot for the parade, was drinking and celebrating with his new friends. My first instinct was to run and join the party, but I knew I'd jeopardize Lumi's cover. Not being able to caress and kiss my Lumi, I did the next best thing, watched and learned. You can buy almost anything in this world; unfortunately, experience is not one of those things. Lumi had me by almost 50 years and those long years had polished Lumi into a shining diamond.

I remember the first time I laid eyes on Lumi. I had just finished my Time Scout training and was getting the tour at KronoCorp. We were walking on the outside hallways of the building, the city sprawled out in front through the full-sized glass walls. There were five of us and our trainer. The trainer was explaining how the rooms work and giving us examples of what some of our first missions might be. Around the bend the most angelic and beautiful face I had ever seen caught my eye. It walked towards us with grace and confidence. The tall figure was fit, strong, and walked like it owned the place. The trainer followed my eyes and once the figure was spotted, we all sat quietly admiring it. Lumi disappeared down the hallway and the guide told us we should all hope one day to be as successful as Lumi.

Ever since that moment I became a fan, eventually a friend, and ultimately Lumi's lover. The problem was that, no matter how bad I wanted or how strongly I loved Lumi, we could never be what I truly wanted us to be. I came back from my daydream to have also lost Lumi. I was bitterly disappointed, decided to call it a night, and started to make my way home. I left the gathering crowd and started swimming upstream like a salmon. More and more people were making their way towards the parade route as the morning was starting to loom.

As I walked I felt a chill down my spine. I quickly stopped and turned, attempting to spot whoever was following me. All I saw was a variety of heads all walking away from me. Pony tails, long hairs, bald heads, blue baseball caps, stocking caps, blonde, brown and even red hair, but no faces tailing me. I wanted to chuck it off to a day of failed endeavors, but my senses were never wrong. Someone was following me, but somehow was eluding me. I gave the sea of heads one last look and went on my way.

I walked and tried to catch whoever was following me, but time after time they eluded me. My mysterious pursuer changed my plans so I made my way through the crowd and headed back to The Sea Urchin. Whoever it was, I had no intention of leading them back to my place. Part of me hoped that it was Mr. Michelson, so I willingly engaged in the cat and mouse game. The crowd started to thin out as I distanced myself from the parade route. Still, whoever was following me kept eluding my attentive eyes. Concern started to grow deep in my stomach in the form of knots. If it had been Mr. Michelson I would have spotted him by now. The options of who was following me became more sinister and worrisome to me. The lessening crowds made me feel exposed now and I picked up the pace.

By the time I made it close to The Sea Urchin, the streets were left only with the drunkenly lost, me, and whoever was still successfully following me. I prepared and readied myself for whoever it might be. I had weaved my way through the streets, I had tried changing direction, and I had already stopped and tied my shoes five times. When the lion hides in the grass waiting for you to make a mistake so it can attack, the best option is to stay still and force it to move.

I stopped, I could see the sign for The Sea Urchin up ahead, but I was done being the mouse in this game. I had picked a spot and I was going to stand there and wait for my lion to make its move. I stood there under the impending dawn and waited. Every second I stood there the streets became more and more empty. I closed my eyes and focused. I could feel the presence, but could not tell exactly where it was. My nose, my eyes, and my ears were failing me in the search for my lion. I kept my eyes closed and reached out with my mind. I could see the street once more, but my eyes remained closed. Everything buzzed and vibrated exuding its specific energy. The silhouettes of the few drunks left on the street vibrated purple. Everything became clear and I searched further and further away from me. That is when I saw it and felt it. The silhouette vibrated in red. I could feel the energy and potential danger coming from it. I was right to be worried. Whoever it was didn't belong here and it knew I didn't either. It was also good enough to elude me until now. I opened my eyes and did the most foolish thing I could do and the one thing the lion would not expect, I started to walk towards it.

I stood at the edge of a dark alley. The buildings rose towards the sky, leaving all but the first 10 feet shadowed in darkness. I peered in and although I could feel the mysterious energy, my eyes could not make out my lion. The trap was laid out, I stood in front of it and decided to enter. The street slowly disappeared behind me as I went deeper into the darkness. The energy buzzed stronger against my skin with every step I took. I was ready to defend myself and put the lion down if need be.

I was close, almost within striking distance, when a bright blinding light attacked my eyes. I sheltered my eyes behind my hands and arms, trying to peek into the bright light. The silhouette was framed by the light now, black and ominous. A familiar and terrifying voice broke the silence.

"What are you doing here, Scout Jordan? The celebration is nowhere near where we are now. What brings you here?" The voice was raspy and powerful. I had heard it many times, we all had, but had never seen the person behind it. The person and the voice stood but a few meters from me and its sheer presence left me paralyzed.

"We have been monitoring your scouting missions and we are not happy with the lack of information. Know that there are two other scouts with you for this event, we will expect as much information from you as we get from them. Consider yourself on notice." The light intensified bringing me to my knees. I hid my eyes in my hands, my face buried on the ground. The energy surged and every cell in my body wanted to scream. The bright light and the darkness disappeared and I was left on my knees and in pain in a normal looking alley. Light illuminated the pavement and the bricks on the walls. The pain slowly dissipated from my body, leaving me confused and concerned.

I sat in the room with the other 5 new scouts, our trainer had left us here for our next lesson. The lights went out in the room and a large screen intensely illuminated before us. The sudden brightness hurt all of our eyes, but we quickly adjusted. An energy filled the room and a dark silhouette broke the plane of the bright screen. It entered from the left, hands clasped behind its back as it slowly walked towards the middle of the screen. The background remained brightly illuminated, but the shape before us remained in complete darkness.

I remember hearing that voice for the first time that day. "Welcome new scouts, today we will learn the boundaries and regulations you must follow. And my personal favorite part, the consequences if these rules are not followed." The shape was facing us and its greeting made me swallow hard. I remember the presentation as the figure grabbed and moved colorful pictures and information around it on the holographic display, while remaining completely engulfed by darkness. The last warning still haunts me to this day. I remember it every time I do what I feel I must do. It was as close as any human could get to experiencing hell on earth. I knew it was one of the risks, but I quickly shoved those memories away and thoughts aside and gathered myself to my feet.

The night was over after that. I was in no mood to hunt or gather data, so I decided to go home. I got to the apartment and didn't even look at the wall of pictures. I lost articles of clothing as I made my way to the bed. By the time I arrived I was naked and plopped down on the soft comfortable bed. As I laid there, I could not help but wonder what would happen if they caught me? I was not worried about myself. I had come to peace with what might happen to me. I worried about Lumi, the most senior scout, and in a relationship with a time changer. I brushed those thoughts aside; if I accomplished what I had sought to do, it would not matter. I found comfort in that thought and allowed myself to rest.

DAY 3

I woke up a couple of hours later, invigorated and ready for what was going to be a very busy and hectic day. The Auditor had made it clear my information was going to be closely scrutinized, so I had to turn a 24 hour day into a 30 hour day, somehow. I took a scalding hot shower and gathered my thoughts. My mind bounced between Mr. Michelson, The Auditor, the parade, and Lumi. I stopped myself before my brain exploded and instead followed a single thread that led to simpler times.

Every new Scout got assigned to a Senior Scout. I was lucky enough to get assigned to the angelic vision from the hallway. When the trainer introduced me to Lumi, all I could do was open my mouth, but no sound came out. The experience, the beauty, and aura of Lumi was that of true royalty amongst the scouts, even back then. Lumi was confident and assertive, but also kind and patient. As we trained in the facility and simulators, Lumi was more than patient in answering my endless barrage of question, always with a smile and encouraging words for me. I was lucky, not only did I learn all that a new Time Scout needed to learn from Lumi, but also learned many tips and tricks that one can only learn from years of experience.

After I had passed all the necessary tests and simulations, I was sent on my first real scouting mission alongside Lumi. We visited an already partially scouted event, but one that still needed more information to ascertain the safety of time tourists. Lumi led me into the training scout room. As we entered the A.I. welcomed us and informed us the time string was ready. I followed Lumi's lead and took a seat on the strange looking reclined chairs. We did one last check of our wrist control units and away we went. No simulation had prepared me for the true rush of traveling through string time and, as most new Scouts, I ended up on my knees throwing up my guts once we arrived.

After fully emptying my insides on the dusty ground, I got the first glimpse of where I was. I knelt on a well packed dirt road surrounded by fields of wheat. The wind gently caressed the wheat, making it dance, creating waves that made the fuzzy fingers greet us. The sun was shining high above us, beating down on my dehydrated body. The cooling breeze made the heat tolerable, slowly returning my composure and strength. Lumi stood beside me with a kind smile and patient eyes. The sun and shadows only accentuated Lumi's true beauty and, for a second or ten, I admired and soaked it all in. Lumi's hand extended towards me, I took it and found my way onto my two feet.

On each side of the road, the fields of wheat extended and danced as far as my eyes could see. Behind us, the road twisted and turned until all that was left of it was a thin line parting the distant fields. Ahead of us was our impressive destination. As the fields of wheat gave way to small wooden houses, those houses gave way to a white marble building, and in the distance, standing tall and proud at the mouth of the port, was the Colossus of Rhodes. In the sun of the midway the impossibly large statue shone and glimmered, making its presence known and imposing to us and any sailor out at sea.

Lumi led the way down the road towards the port city and the Colossus. I felt awkward wearing only what appeared to be a decorated white blanket and some rudimentary leather sandals before we left. As we entered the city the strange clothing made perfect sense. The year was 280 BC and the giant bronze Colossus had just been finished. Today was going to be the day of celebration for its completion and the commemoration of the victory over Antigonus I, Monophthalmus, and Cyprus. The city was preparing for a large festival to honor Helios the Colossus. Helios was driving the sun to its highest point in the sky and the festivities were about to begin.

We could hear the rumble of the people as we approached the festival. At first I could not make out what they were saying, but as Lumi reassured me, eventually my ears and my brain caught up and I could understand their language. Not only could I understand it, when offered a cup filled with mead, I was able to answer properly. We joined the celebration and it was an amazing day. As the sun began to set over the Mediterranean Sea, the festivities just intensified. Torches and lamps were lit and even in darkness the Colossus stood tall and proud. It was a great achievement of technology. It stood 30 meters and it let the ancient world know that the gods watched over these people. The statue would have been a sight to behold even back in my time.

The crowd got a little wilder and a little less dressed, but the festivities remained friendly. The women who kept refilling our cups of mead, under the influence themselves of the fermented nectar, decided to make Lumi and I their targets of lust. Two of them came to us and were facing us as we leaned against the white marble walls of a beautiful temple. We stood outside under the light of the stars, the galaxy leaving its white streak of burning suns across the infinite dark skies. The torches lit the grounds, but the universe illuminated the skies. It was a clear night and the moon was but a sliver allowing the stars to shine for once. The two beautiful women stood in front of us this time without the pitchers that they had been hauling around all night. The children had been sent to bed, some of them under the effect of the mead, and now only the adults remained. Everyone was joyous and seemed to want to finish the night with a bang.

Both of them had beautiful black hair, their skin darkened by the sun to a beautiful brown, and their eyes as dark as the night's sky. Although the individual parts of their faces were different, their totality showed they were sisters. They had worked hard and celebrated all night making all of the citizens inebriated and they were trying to make us their reward. They approached us with smiles on their faces and lust in their eyes. Once in front of us, they exchanged a look and their hands slowly removed the white piece of fabric covering their chests. The tunics fell to their waists only held there by the piece of decorative rope that was accentuating their curves. Their breasts lay exposed and the seas cold breeze made them even more alluring. Their walk had turned into a stalk as they finished closing the distance between their half-naked bronzed bodies and us.

I swallowed hard and looked at Lumi. No simulation had prepared me for a situation like this. Lumi gave me that comforting smile and we both turned our attention back to our half naked predators. Lumi uttered one phrase. At the time it was the truth and seemed completely innocent. It wasn't until I did more research at what it meant when we returned, that I truly understood the implications of what he said.

"Thank you ladies, but he is my pupil," Lumi's voice was strong and confident. The moment the women heard him, they first exchanged a look with each other, then looked back and forth between Lumi and me. They smiled and their smiles held so many unspoken words. Holding our gaze, they bowed at the waist, turned and went off to hunt other prey with their exposed breasts. I was puzzled at their reaction and tried to get an explanation out of Lumi. For the first time I was not able to get an answer to one of my questions, instead, told to research it once we got back. I could have sworn I had seen Lumi blush that night and it took nearly 17 years for it to be admitted. That had not only been my first scouting mission, it had also been our first "date".

Something happened that night amongst the half-naked women, mead, and a Colossus between Lumi and me. I could not call it love, I had seen true love many years back in a blood covered forest, and I would never be lucky enough to feel it. But it was our version of it, unintentionally we had started down the path of partners, one that would lead to 53 wonderful, but sorrow filled years to this day.

The bathroom was but a cloud now and the unrelenting hot water kept beating on my head and back. I was smiling at the beautiful memory as I leaned on the cool wall tile. I loved the feeling between the scalding hot water and the cooling tile and every time I had the chance to experience it I would indulge. The temperature of the water was starting to cool as I had apparently used it all up. I shut off the water, dried off, and made my way to the kitchen. I filled myself with some 21st century delicious food and got ready to head to the parade. I didn't know what ever became of Mr. Michelson last night and he would have to wait today for a bit. There was no way I could miss the parade now. I got dressed with more Cubs paraphernalia and headed out. The morning was cold and it took me a few seconds to adjust to the temperature after my hot shower. As I walked, I debated where I should go to experience the parade, but while my mind lied to itself, my feet led me to where I had last seen Lumi. My eyes, listening to my feet and not my brain, were scanning the crowd for the familiar face. After a short search, I spotted Lumi once more smiling and melting the people around. The alcohol had disappeared as uniformed cops brought order for the parade. The streets buzzed with anticipation just like the small Greek island once had. The gods had changed, but the excitement and need to celebrate their idols hadn't. The parade was about to start and the streets had been blocked off. I wanted nothing more than to cross and share another historic moment with my Lumi, but couldn't.

Being that close, yet not being able to share the moment with Lumi grew increasingly frustrating. In order to properly enjoy the festivities, I decided to head north and find another spot where I could actually watch the parade instead of staring at Lumi hoping to exchange eye contact. I tried to walk through the crowd, but it was more like squeezing my way through it. The streets were filled and more kept piling in from the side streets. After a few blocks the crowd was so thick that I could no longer travel. I found a good spot and killed time watching the excited crowd. Beers were replaced with coffee cups in the hands of the humanity sprawled alongside of me. People sipped the hot elixir and plumes of steam escaped their lungs after each sip.

Between the smiles and the plumes of steam, Helios smiled upon me, and I saw another familiar and elusive face. I had passed right by Mr. Michelson without noticing him as I squeezed my way through the thick crowd. He was 20 meters or so back in the direction I had come from. He was out of his suit and was wearing a Cubs jersey like most of the crowd. His change of clothes didn't surprise me as much as the companions with him.

As always there was a beautiful woman hanging all over him, but the way she looked at him was different. It wasn't lust in her eyes, it was love.

She looked at him then at the young boy straddling his shoulders. The boy had to be six or seven years old. He was well-bundled and his excited eyes scanned the streets for the parade. His face was filled with pride and happiness as he stood there that cold October morning. The woman by him leaned in close to him, wrapping her arm around his back and hiding her hand in his back pocket for warmth. His hands held onto the feet of the young boy whose face was indistinguishably a younger version of his.

I knew he had a family, but seeing him as an actual family man angered me for some reason. He was a monster and mistake for me to erase, and to see that joy in his face was unacceptable. I took a moment and relaxed my clenched jaw. I could not spend the whole parade focused on him, so I decided to focus on the child. His eyes were glassy in the cold morning air and his spirit encapsulated the feelings of the whole city. He kept scanning the crowd and soaking in every burst of color and motion. His poor neck was going to be exhausted after moving his head back and forth over and over, trying to see everything.

As the crowd south of us began to roar, his head quickly snapped in that direction, and stood fixated on the street. The parade had begun and the noise escalated. The first bit of confetti started to rain on us propelled by the wind. In the distance I could see the first vehicle and the crowd exploded. The woman with Mr. Michelson checked the little boy's ears and I could see bright orange foam ear plugs stuck inside of them. The boy shook off his mother's hands and freed himself so that he could catch every second of the parade.

A wave of hands formed as everyone eagerly tried to catch the small trinkets that the players and team were throwing into the crowd. The boy kept reaching and missing until finally one of the well bundled players threw him a collar of blue beads and the boy caught it. There was music, there was cheering, the players would stop and thank the fans over loud speakers and even the skies shone bright and warm for the occasion. I watched the parade through the eyes of that child, a child whose father I had to take away from him. For a second I started to feel sympathy for Mr. Michelson and his child, then I quickly remembered the incident at the lake and those thoughts were washed away.

The parade lasted well into the early afternoon. Once done, the crowd rushed to all the open restaurants and after their tummies were filled, the celebration kicked into high gear. I picked up some fusion food from one of the many food trucks that were patrolling around like vultures. I didn't feel like following Mr. Michelson back home with his happy family, so I ate and headed towards The Sea Urchin.

I could only eat about half the overcomplicated burrito, so I threw the other half away. I soaked in the crowd, looking at every detail, trying to record as much information as possible as I walked. I caught myself smiling several times and it reminded me how much I actually enjoyed what I did. I had been bred for it, but the satisfaction was real none the less. Most of the families had cleared out of the streets as beer and other bottled drinks started to make themselves more visible. The police lingered around corners, making sure nothing got out of hand, but understanding that stopping the celebrations would probably lead to riots.

As I approached the next corner, a scene for the ages unfolded before my very own eyes. A well lubricated fan handed one of the police officers on the corner a beer. I cringed as he did it and expected an arrest, instead the police officer smiled, they toasted, and drank their beer. The happy man went on his way and the police officer laughed and shrugged as he and his partner recounted what just happened. This was truly a very special celebration, in a very interesting city, with very happy fans. Once we cleared it as safe, I was pretty sure this would become a very popular vacation destination.

I received two free drinks as I finished my walk to The Sea Urchin. I accepted them and drank them without concern, the joys of being immune to toxins. The celebration spilled into the Urchin, so I felt comfortable taking residence there and watching the crowd. Mike welcomed me with his usual nod and I found my way to a booth inside the not so crowded bar. The rum and cokes started arriving and didn't stop for the rest of the night. What I would have given to feel even a buzz as they call it.

People circled in and out of The Sea Urchin, most of them didn't stay for long. They drank their drinks and left after Mike's friendly service. I sat, drank, and enjoyed the never ending carousel. I was gambling that once Mr. Michelson was done playing domestic he would venture this way to hunt. After a few hours of waiting, my patience was rewarded. Mr. Michelson walked through the door with a swagger and confidence that no one else in this fine establishment had. Most of the women stopped and peered over their drinks in his direction, even the obviously taken ones. Surprisingly, a few gentlemen did the same, even ones I would not have guessed would be interested in the likes of him.

I remained hidden in my dark booth and watched him walk and take residence at his usual table. He carefully scanned the crowd, and the shadows protected me from his searching eyes. Undetected, I was able to watch and study Mr. Michelson. His body language was completely different from the one of the man I had seen earlier. While at the parade, his body was relaxed and moved with grace and joy. The man I had just watched enter the bar and sit at his table, moved like a predator. He made me think of a lion gracefully but menacingly stalking his way through the savannah. He was the apex predator in here and moved with an energy acknowledging that he knew it. His movements were sensuous, provocative, and menacing. His aura oozed sexuality and hunger. I could completely understand why women threw themselves at him. It was this energy, this aura that made him so attractive and terrifying. If he wasn't stopped, he could go on forever seducing and killing women.

His searching eyes spotted a possible prize. He stood from his table and strode through the sticky dirty floor, making his way to the bar. The poor girl sitting there had been staring at him since he walked in. Unable to pass up easy and wounded prey, he pursued her. I called her a girl, but she was really a woman. She had to be in her late thirties or early forties, but was holding up very well for her age. She was voluptuous and curvy and not shy about sharing it with the world. As he approached, she looked at him as if she was the predator, but the poor gal didn't know who she was dealing with. She smiled and seductively licked her exaggerated red lips. Her blonde hair was expertly styled and poofed by too much product. She wore a Cubs jersey which she so happened to leave unbuttoned so that her long cleavage could be admired in its entirety. She left little to the imagination and her matching blue bra more than peeked out in several spots. Below her jersey was a skirt that barely peeked out from under it.

She rode the line between temptress and desperate so tightly that depending on the angle, I kept changing my mind about her. She had plenty of jewelry, but no wedding ring in sight. Her heavily made up face gave Mr. Michelson her most seductive smile as he approached her. She thought she had the fish on the hook, while in reality, she might end up becoming chum. I thought about intervening, but this clash of the titans was too good to pass up watching.

He reached her and instantly closed the personal space between them. He leaned strong and tall with one elbow against the bar, squeezing his body between hers and the other occupied bar stool. She finished erasing the distance between them with a playful caress of his chest as they exchanged smile-filled words. He instantly signaled Mike to bring another drink to the lady. Mike smiled in acknowledgement, then rolled his eyes as Mr. Michelson directed his attention back to the voluptuous blonde.

The colorful martini arrived and their conversation continued for a few more minutes. It was abruptly interrupted by a balding man coming back from the bathroom. He must have been in his early forties, but looked worse for wear. He approached the incredibly close lovebirds and reprimanded the flirty blonde. She turned her attention towards the balding man. He was short and stocky with maybe 10 hairs all reaching in different directions on top of his head. He wore a matching jersey to hers, but his was struggling to keep all of him inside of it. The buttons screamed for their lives every time he took a breath in and his large stomach expanded. He was neither graceful nor seductive, but judging by the large and expensive watch on his wrist, which was what, attracted her to him.

As the balding man reprimanded her, she clung to him, kissing his neck and whispering things into his ear. After the secrets she whispered into his ear, he pulled back away from her and started to look and back and forth between her and Mr. Michelson. Mr. Michelson stood his ground, still sharing personal space with the voluptuous blonde and looking as sexy and arrogant as always. As the balding man kept looking back and forth, Mr. Michelson shot him a smile full of innuendos. The balding man stumbled a couple of steps back and screamed, "Screw this", loud enough for me to hear over the murmur of the crowd, and left the bar.

Without any hesitation, the blonde turned her full attention back to Mr. Michelson. She grabbed onto the middle of his jersey with both hands. She had lost her rich whale for the night and she was not about to lose Mr. Michelson. She leaned into him, their faces no more than a few inches away as they talked. Their lips enunciated every word as if they were saying dirty and naughty things. Fake laughs and giggles were being exchanged as their bodies became as close as possible while in a public space.

He leaned in to her, his face getting buried in her blonde hair, and his mouth whispered something into her ear. Her smile vanished as her teeth bit on her lower lip. Her back arched and her large breasts pushed forward and into his body. He grabbed her by her hand and she quickly complied. He led her by her wrist and her quick and eager steps did their best to obediently follow him.

My amusement was replaced by concern. He was leading her to the back entrance and possibly to her death. I had to admit I was surprised at his choice. He preferred the young and naïve type, neither which this voluptuous woman was. I didn't want him to spot me as they made their way to the back of the bar, but I could not lose them either. Once he entered the back hallway, I rushed from my dark booth to catch up with them. By the time I made it to the hallway they were nowhere in sight. I stormed out the back door just to stare at an empty and dirty alley.

I stood quietly listening for any signs of a muffled struggle, but all I heard were a few rats scurrying about. The alley was long in both directions, there was no way he led her away that fast. Foiled once more by Mr. Michelson, I went back in to the Urchin just to be surprised by the noises coming from the bathroom. I had heard of loud sex, but this woman was making sure everyone knew she was having sex with Mr. Michelson. Her moans and screams made it sound like someone was being murdered in the bathroom, but her constant request for more made it clear she was safe. I could not help but to laugh as I walked my way back to my booth.

The screaming and moaning continued, loud enough to be heard over murmur of the people in the bar. I giggled my way back to my booth as the bar became more and more quiet. People were starting to look around trying to figure out what the origin of the screams and moans were. I once more hid in the darkness of the booth and enjoyed watching the scene unfold. One by one the patrons of The Sea Urchin became quiet, until all that could be heard were the loud love noises coming from the bathroom. Smiles blossomed on the faces of the patrons as juvenile looks started to be exchanged. Mike shook his head in mild disapproval and continued to clean glasses behind the bar. As the last climatic yell escaped the bathroom, giggling overtook the listening crowd. After a few moments of silence, the blonde emerged from the bathroom, grinning from ear to ear and dragging Mr. Michelson by the wrist. Her eyes were glassy and her hair not as perfectly styled as when she went into the bathroom.

A group of well inebriated young men started to slowly clap as the couple emerged from the bathroom. More joined in the clapping until it became a thunderous ovation. Yelping and whooping followed and the blonde graciously waved to the crowd smiling, proud of her conquest. Once settled on the barstool, the clapping subsided and everyone went back to their interrupted conversations, although now everyone was still smiling. Mr. Michelson seemed pretty ambivalent about what just happened. He sat next to the blonde at the bar as she clung on to him for dear life. She was proud of her conquest and now she wanted to gloat.

THE SIMPLE THINGS

Hunger struck me as my stomach rumbled. It had been a while since I had eaten and I needed to refuel. The only food in the bar was stale peanuts, so I was going to have to wander elsewhere to quiet my stomach. I did have one weakness and it was the delicious taste of food. I had been waiting for the right moment to visit the restaurant across from the Sea Urchin and that moment had arrived. I looked out the window and could see the green neon sign dancing and calling out to me. I looked back at Mr. Michelson and the still grinning blonde and felt pretty safe he was not going to go anywhere. She was all over him and I was fairly certain she would keep guard of him for me. I looked back out the window and imagined how delicious the food across the street might be and my choice was made.

I carefully exited the bar making sure Mr. Michelson didn't see me. I succeeded and the night welcomed me with a cold slap to the face. The temperature had dropped and my Jersey didn't provide much refuge. I checked the street before crossing, but the only dangerous things on it were a few very drunk celebrating fans. The sign above the entrance, entranced my eyes. It was a cartoon jalapeño and the lights flashing on and off made it look as if it were dancing. I could smell the delicious food that awaited me inside of it and followed my stomach into the hole-in-the-wall restaurant.

Most scouts would limit themselves to just water and wait to eat once back from their missions. I, on the other hand, had developed an incredible appetite and curiosity for new foods. Maybe it was part of my genetic makeup or maybe it was an addiction formed when tasting the foods back in the redwood forest. Either way, I could not help myself. I bypassed the rations waiting for me during checkups and took advantage of any delicious food I could find during my missions. At first, my epicurean adventures had been frowned upon, but I had convinced the supervisors at KronoCorp that it was its own version of tourism. So far, very few tourists had been brave enough to take the culinary vacation, but it gave me the license to keep trying new and delicious foods.

As soon as I walked into the restaurant the kaleidoscope of smells overwhelmed my senses. The smells of spices and cooking meats felt warming to my soul. I joined the line of hungry guests and tried to decide what to order from the overhead menu. The menu hung over the counter and was peppered with pictures of some of the delicious dishes one could order. I took step after step as my feet led me to the ordering counter. Once there, a young man with a thick accent welcomed me and asked me for my order. I tried to decide many times during my slow shuffle to the counter what I wanted to experience. I had made my choice at least ten times and still, as I stood in front of the young man, I didn't know what to order. As always, my indecision and curiosity for what hid behind the kitchen led me to order a large quantity of plates. I ordered six different things and the young man asked me if it were to go. I corrected him and told him it was for here. He asked if I wanted something to drink and I requested water.

I wanted to be able to savor each bite without the adulteration of some sugary drink. Once I paid, I was told I was number 67 and was handed a small plastic cup. I stepped to the side, found the soda machine and filled my cup with water. I found a chair by the front windows, although I was about to be distracted by my taste buds, I wanted to keep an eye on The Sea Urchin in case Mr. Michelson decided to leave. Every time a number got called out from behind the counter I quickly twitched to get up, even though it wasn't mine. As I sat I kept reminding myself of 67, 67, 67, 67 and listened attentively as I looked out of the window to The Sea Urchin. Number after number kept getting called and the anticipation was killing me. I could feel my mouth salivating and my stomach demanding I fill it. Sixty-seven was finally called and I about jumped out of my stool. I calmed myself, walked over to the counter where two trays filled with food awaited me. It should have taken me two trips, but I grabbed each tray with one hand and made my way back to my table where the lonely cup of water awaited me. The guys behind the counter exchanged a few words regarding how much food I had ordered and a few eyes followed my balancing odyssey.

Finally back at the table, I arranged all of the plates in front of me and allowed my eyes a second to soak in the bounty before me. I held myself back from just diving in and experiencing flavors and textures. Instead, I sat there and admired all the food in front of me. I made a plan of action on how I would taste and devour every single morsel. Once I had teased myself enough and had a plan in place, I dove in. Every single crunchy, cheesy, savory, spicy, and delicious bite brought out feelings in me that food shouldn't. I went from one dish to the other and back again. I figured which one was my favorite and left it for last. I wanted it to be the last thing I tasted. I kept my eye on The Sea Urchin, every time the door opened I paused and made sure Mr. Michelson wasn't leaving the fine establishment. Once I determined it wasn't him, I would go back to my feast. It took a while, but I consumed and savored all of the six dishes. A different young man came to my table to remove the plates once I was done and his eyes opened wide in pure amazement. He smiled and removed the evidence of my gluttony and went back into the kitchen. As soon as he entered the hoots and hollers begun, all of them amazed at my gastronomic prowess.

I finished my little cup of water and left the Dancing Jalapeño. The cold night air actually felt refreshing after all the spicy food. I made my way back to The Sea Urchin as the streets were filling up more and more with lubricated celebrators. The crowd was thick and friendly and the alcohol in their veins was keeping them warm. I walked into a now crowded Urchin and Mr. Michelson was right where I left him. The blonde had done a good job of guarding him for me.

He noticed me as I walked in and I smiled at him. The blonde noticed and grabbed on to her prize a little tighter. He could not help but to smile back at me as his face disappeared behind the blonde's head. I had baited him; hopefully, he would take the hook tonight. I made my way to an open booth and made sure to walk as sexy as possible on my way there. My smile had grabbed his attention, I wanted my swaying hips to make him come crawling to me. I nodded to Mike and soon his masculine sister brought me my usual. Instead of sipping on the drink I sucked on the tiny bar straw very provocatively, while looking at Mr. Michelson. Eventually, he saw me and seeing my lips the poor man blushed.

The blonde was losing steam as well. Drink after drink was starting to take a toll on her. She was hanging on to Mr. Michelson not for seduction, but for balance. Soon enough she would pass out in a corner somewhere or be taken home by some desperate soul. Then Mr. Michelson would certainly come hunting for me.

I had to give it to the old bar fly, she was a resilient one. It took almost 3 hours of hard drinking before she was passed out on the bar. Even in her drunken and debilitated state, she would not let go of Mr. Michelson and he seemed to be fine getting all of her attention. Apparently, a family day left the man a little desperate for lustful attention. Once she was somehow being held up by the bar and the stool she sat on, he broke away from her charming embrace.

His eyes once more found me and his smile tried to charm me. I smiled back. I had about all of the celebrating people watching as I could handle for a day. I wanted him to make his move. Time was becoming of the essence and after tomorrow night, I would have to return. Receiving my reciprocating smile, he causally strutted over to my darkened booth.

"May I join you?" he asked and his voice almost purred like a tiger. I worked up my best blush and nodded with wide eyes.

"I thought you had forgotten about me." I pouted, making him smile even wider.

"No, how could I forget about a beauty like you? I have just been preoccupied with other engagements." He tried to smile innocently, but his eyes betrayed him. Even though I knew better, I played along and kept gushing as he took a seat across from me in the booth.

He gracefully deposited himself on the cushioned and torn vinyl seat of the booth. He held my gaze as he moved, like a predator keeping their eye on their unassuming prey. I knew that look, I had been on the receiving end of it many a time already, and I was glad I was finally getting it from him.

I remember the first time I got that look. I was actually a little scared when I was on the receiving end of predator eyes. I must say I find it a little amusing now. Now that I think about it, it wasn't that long ago. The year was 1996 and his name had been Eric Ferguson. He was a police officer, well in title at least, but in reality he was in the dawn of what would become a string of 30 plus murders. He liked to prey on prostitutes, arrest them, do what he pleased with them, then dispose of them. He worked in the Las Vegas police department and prostitutes, being transient, and disappearing in that city during that time didn't really raise much suspicion. It wasn't until his final would-be victim got away, that the truth of what kind of monster he really was, was revealed.

I had commissioned a scouting mission to Las Vegas and knew it was my chance to erase him. I had been a scout for 8 years and had elaborately worked out my plans on how I would proceed with my mission. Eric Ferguson was just starting, according to my estimates he had only about 2 victims so far.

If I could stop him it would save a few lives, but more importantly, start to slowly change the ripples in my time.

The scouting mission was to take two weeks. It was the middle of the summer and one of the most renowned old Las Vegas casinos was closing, the Sands. It was the end of an era from old Las Vegas to the New Vegas. So of course we were going to scout it for the nostalgic and gambling inclined time tourist. The hotel was to be imploded and I must admit, it was quite the spectacle.

Anyways it gave me the opportunity to go after my first target. I was nervous and scared of what would happen if I were discovered, but my mind was set and I was going to go through with it. It took me almost a whole week from my two week scouting mission to find Eric Ferguson and to get him to take notice. I had never had to pretend to be a prostitute, but I adjusted quickly. My good looks made him take me for a novice, a transient, and I was instantly an easy target for him. I remember the night he decided to make his move, I had baited him and he drove head first into my trap.

He picked me up on Riviera Boulevard, cuffed me for the second time, and instead of driving me to the police station, he started to drive east out into the desert. I asked every question he would have expected me to ask, further baiting him and pushing him to try to make me his victim. By the time we made it out to the desolate dry spot he had chosen, I had worked myself free of the handcuffs. I remember him pulling me out of the patrol car so desperately and seeing those eyes for the first time. They were eyes filled with a need so primal and so raw that it was like truly looking into someone's soul. All the shades came down, all the filters disappeared, and all the niceties of society evaporated. The only thing left in those eyes was a need, a raw energy so primal that not even the genetic advancements of my civilization had been able to eradicate.

I remember falling into those eyes as if they were an infinite crevasse. There was something so terrifying in them, but yet so beautiful. I was staring into the true and naked soul of another human being, and it was wonderful. For the first time I understood what it meant to be human. In that darkness behind those eyes I saw the truth of what we were and what we should be. It made my decision to erase Eric Ferguson that night even easier. Carrying it out proved a little more interesting than I would have cared for.

He was so lost in his darkness he didn't even notice my hands were now free. To fulfill the part, I was dressed in a short zebra striped mini skirt dress, high heels, oversized hoop earrings and colorful, awfully applied makeup. He grabbed me by the arm and tossed me on top of the hood of his patrol car. The headlights illuminated the darkness of the desert. It was a warm night, still being late June. The stars twinkled above and the headlights teased infinite sands. I could have ended him right there, but I wanted to learn as much as possible, so I played along until I had to act.

He grabbed me by the neck and made me horrible promises of what he was planning to do with a filthy slut like me, including pissing over the shallow grave he was planning to bury me in. I had prepared and studied and acted how I knew he expected a victim to act. Then came the moment of revelation which forced me to make my move and erase Eric Ferguson. The moment he lifted my skirt, was the moment his predatory eyes were replaced by fear and confusion.

In the quest for genetic perfection and perfect Utopian society,

Civilization had sacrificed a lot; in my opinion too much. Genetic modification had evolved from disease resistance, to aesthetics, to the attempt to create the perfect human. In a misguided search for equality and the elimination of violent crimes, humanity decided to forsake what made us the most human. We forsake our genders, sex, and procreation. Since we could design and grow humans in laboratories, the middle man was eliminated altogether. Along with it, the necessity for sex, traditional procreation, gender and sexual organs. The end result were us, me. Generation after generation of Unix, with no sexual organs, more beautiful than any other permutation of humanity, receiver of complete lust, but unable to ever experience or enjoy it.

It was the norm, what was right and what was best for all of us. That was until I visited the Randoms and since then I knew better. I had been designed and created to be a superior human, along with everyone in civilization, but in reality we were barely human any more, and I hoped to fix that.

My lack of genitalia more than caught Eric Ferguson by surprise, he kept groping and feeling, wanting to find the familiar wetness and softness of a female vagina. Instead, in front of him stood the most beautiful "woman" he had ever seen, but who wasn't a woman whatsoever. He kept feeling at the soft and smooth patch of skin where my humanity should have been. Genitals like many other "useless" organs, no longer lived in our bodies.

He kept feeling and hoping it was all a logistical mistake of his fingers, but then my eyes revealed the truth to him. My expression changed and I was no longer playing the role of the victim. He had fallen into my trap and now struggled to get out. He backed away and called me every insult he could muster while drawing his gun on me.

"What are you? You some sort of alien?" His eyes were now wide, his figure lit by the headlights of the patrol car. "Explain yourself! Or I will shoot you right this second!"

I stood there and carefully studied the transformation. What once had been a predator now stood before me terrified and confused. He should have tried to shoot me, but he fought to remain in control by demanding his questions be answered. I stood there and found myself smirking at his panic. I hadn't expected that, but I embraced it. The smirk turned into a smile as I started to walk toward the terrified cop. He kept waving his gun around in the air, pointing it at me, but his fear made the metal weight waver and shake in his hands. For every two steps I took he took another step back, until he was starting to reach the end of the power of the headlights. His feet stopped and he once more demanded I explain myself. My smile widened as I became the predator and his exhausted arms and shaking fingers pulled the first round. Time slowed, but the bullet wasn't even close. It shot up in the air and into the stars. I advanced quickly and disarmed the man. When time caught up, he stood there confused with empty hands and a look of total despair.

As a last resort he reached for the radio on his shoulder, only to be met with static and silence. I took the clip out and disarmed the gun as he kept screaming into the black plastic box on his shoulder. I tossed the parts of the gun into the silent darkness and directed my attention back to the now defenseless Eric Ferguson.

His shouts and demands ceased as he searched within for a solution to his predicament. After much searching, he stood still staring at his boots. He didn't move and if it weren't for the slow back and forth swaying, I would have thought he was asleep. I stood and watched, absorbing every second of his behavior. After his long pause, he either decided to stop playing possum or figured out his next course of action. His eyes met my gaze once more and he demanded, "Who and what are you, I will not ask again?"

He had dug deep and filled himself with the false courage we gather when in reality we are scared shitless. His eyes were full of rage and he was converting that rage into courage. The behavior was fascinating. He reached to his belt and pulled out a short metal rod. He snapped it in the air and it made a sequence of ever deeper clicks as the baton extended to length. He found some resolve and started to walk towards me as he elevated the metal baton. His eyes were so full of rage that tears had begun to stream down his cheeks. He was cornered and scared, but he was going to go down with a fight.

There wasn't much of a fight. Eric Ferguson's body lay lifeless at my feet in the quiet desert night. His eyes still beaded with tears, but they stared into the infinite darkness of space. I stood there with his body at my feet and the weight of distant stars above my head. I didn't know what I should be feeling and what was ok to feel. I had broken the man's neck. Lives were saved and I had started to make a difference towards a different present for myself. I should have felt bad, but I didn't. I had resolve in me for what I was doing. I wished that second I had felt something and that it had been the right thing to feel. Instead, I stood there empty and worried about the next task.

I buried the body like he had planned to do with me and drove the patrol car back to the city. I left the cruiser a ball of fire and went back to my scouting. As I walked away, I still didn't feel anything about what I had just done. Still to this day I haven't, I don't know if it should worry me or if I should be proud of my focus. Only time will tell.

FRAGILE EGOS

The conversation with Mr. Michelson progressed and I knew he was getting close to making his move. Unlike last time, I noticed he didn't buy me a single drink. He wanted me sober, he wanted me to know what was happening, and he wanted to feed on my horror. Some like the control, some like the challenge. I had figured out what had been my mistake with Mr. Michelson the first night. The man had everything he could want; he didn't want a willing victim. What he craved was a challenge.

Finally knowing what my hunter sought, I adjusted and gave it to him. The conversation switched from me gushing and flirting, to witty and sarcastic. His already hungry eyes really lit up and came to life then. We talked for a few hours and the zingers bounced back and forth. I had him and was reeling him in. Once his eyes were filled with need I decided to tell him good night. I tried to excuse myself to go home, but he was not having any part of it. After much insisting, I agreed to let him walk me home.

As we excited The Sea Urchin, the streets were still crowded with now mostly drunk celebrants. We both weaved our way through the crowd next to each other. There was noise and chanting, but our attention was solely focused on each other. Two predators hunting each other; both pretending to be lambs.

That is when I saw it out of the corner of my eye. I should have been able to react, done something about it, but all I could do was watch as it unfolded. The figure moved fast and, with one swift bump, destroyed the house of cards trap I had been drawing Mr. Michelson into. The blue Cubs jersey blurred through my vision and placed a stiff shoulder right into Mr. Michelson's chest. The hollow thud broke our dance through the crowd. Mr. Michelson tried to move along, but the other party was in the mood for more. Fighting back the urge to intervene, I allowed Mr. Michelson to take care of the situation.

The other man was smaller in stature than him. Maybe a primal display of dominance would seal the deal for us tonight. I took a step back and allowed Mr. Michelson to establish his dominance in the concrete jungle. I could see his face and the back of our assailant was to me. The smaller man wore a Cubs hat facing backwards the red capital C stitched in the blue head ware. The smaller man shoved Mr. Michelson without much success. The larger and stronger man smiled and shoved him back, but his grin disappeared when he could not move the smaller assailant. The shoving was a stalemate, so fists started to fly.

The whole time I could see Mr. Michelson's face and judged from his expression how well or poorly the fight was going. The strange blue dressed man did a very good job of keeping his back towards me and separating me from Mr. Michelson. Many a punch flew, very few landed, and both men did a very good job of avoiding each other's strikes. The frustration in Mr. Michelson's face grew with each missed punch. Eventually, his frustration turned to pain as a few punches from the blue man landed on his stomach and face. Mr. Michelson fell to the ground holding his torso, not being able to breathe. I readied myself to act, but the blue assailant turned and started to walk away, his job apparently done.

I rushed to the aid of Mr. Michelson, but his pride was more hurt than any part of his anatomy. My chances with him tonight had walked away with the blue man. I looked in the direction of the man that spoiled my evening. The face under the blue hat was looking back at us as it walked away. I recognized the beautiful eyes and the immaculate face. I had an eternal second to soak in who I was looking at. I wanted to shout, but the incalculable amount of questions that burst inside my head left me paralyzed. Lumi met my gaze before turning and disappearing into the crowd.

I stood frozen, staring into the crowd, in the meantime Mr. Michelson gathered himself and got to his feet. He made a noise with his throat to snap me out of my trance. His eyes were filled with shame when I looked back into them. He quickly looked away and disappeared, cursing. "What the hell was that?!"

He continued to ramble and posture trying to find his pride somewhere in his words. I let him get it all out of his system; I had my own questions on what had just happened. Why had Lumi intervened? Was Lumi protecting me? Was I about to get caught by the Auditor? Why wouldn't Lumi talk to me, instead taking such harsh action? The questions kept, going and going in my mind. Mr. Michelson noticed I was no longer paying attention to his rant and directed his attention back to me.

"I'm sorry for the outburst, but that guy just surprised me. He moved like a fighter, he must be a fighter, otherwise he would have stood no chance." I smiled and played along, poor Mr. Michelson didn't realize he never stood a chance with Lumi. It was a killer whale against a seal pup; Lumi was just playing with Mr. Michelson.

Whatever Lumi was trying to disrupt, worked. The mood was dead now, after a few more blocks of walking and talking, Mr. Michelson and I said our goodbyes and he went on his way. I feverishly tried to convince him not to leave, but how was he supposed to play lion when he felt like a mouse. I gave up on what might have been my last chance and went home. I could only hope that I would run into him tomorrow, my last day, again. Otherwise, I might have to break my own protocol and kill him in cold blood.

Defeated and with nowhere else to go, I found my way back to my apartment. I could have gone back to base, but after what just happened with Lumi, there was no way I was going back, until I knew I would not be arrested on site. I made my way to my apartment. I replayed in my head all the events since the moment I had arrived. Had I made a crucial mistake? Had the Auditor figured out my side venture? What was Lumi trying to protect me from or warn me about?

I spent the rest of the night combing over my notes, both the ones I reported and the ones I kept to myself. There was nothing I could find. I had been careful as always. The only different thing was that Lumi was along for the same scouting. I guess Mr. Michelson was going to be my 30th erased killer. All the faces flashed in front of me as I thought about it. Not the pictures, but the faces of all those monsters as I took their life away. That moment when their eyes went from showing so many emotions at once, to when they became glassy and empty like fish at the market. All those faces flashed and rushed through my mind, over and over. The cycle would continue until I decided to stop it. I let the faces and the eyes keep circulating, I needed to remember and truly appreciate all the good I was doing.

Lumi interrupted my mental stroll down memory lane. Lumi stood in front of me and I hadn't realized it. "Jordan!"

I snapped out of it. In front of me stood Lumi, with an expression I had never seen before on that beautiful face. Lightning whipped through the air and thunder rumbled in the night's sky, making me jump. The beginning of the end of the celebrations had begun. It hadn't been exhaustion or the police. In the end, the only thing that could stop Chicago celebrating for the Cubs was Mother Nature.

After the whiplash sound of lightning, rain began to fall, filling the air with its relaxing noise and ozone smell. Lumi stood there looking around at my exposed bounty of pictures. Lumi had an idea of what I was trying to do, but didn't really know. I guess the cat was out of the bag completely now.

"Who are all these people?" Lumi's eyes jumped from one picture to the next, horrified and never meeting my eyes.

"You know who they are. It is what I must do to fix things." As I said it I could see Lumi's body recoil under my words. For the first time I felt like the monster and I did not like it. I stood up and started to pick up the pictures off the table, leaving Lumi staring into the infiniteness of the wood grain.

"There are so many, Jordan, and nothing has changed." Lumi pointed out an ugly truth I had been ignoring as I put away the pictures in my box. There had been many. I had expected more ripples to have made it through the corridors of time. Instead, things had remained pretty much the same.

I pushed away doubt and proceeded to get up close to Lumi. I went in for a kiss, just to be rejected. "What were you planning to do with that man tonight?"

I took a step back and considered how to answer Lumi's question. "You know what I had to do."

Before I could say another word, Lumi snapped. I had never seen Lumi this way and it bothered me more than I thought. "You have to stop. It is not working, Jordan. The Auditor has taken notice of you. I can't protect you anymore. Please I beg you, just be happy with me and be done."

Lumi's eyes welled up with tears; I had never seen such raw emotion and desperation out of Lumi. My heart broke, but my resolve held strong. I remembered all the dead bodies in the forest. It wasn't the faces of the adults that haunted me. It was the faces of all the children staining the grass with their crimson blood, as their dead eyes stared off into the canopy of the giant redwoods. As many lives as I had erased it didn't even come close to the hundreds that expired that day. Trying to change the tide of humanity was not going to be an easy endeavor and I had just started.

I looked into Lumi's desperate eyes. They were begging me, imploring me to stop. Lumi's face showed a being that was broken and exhausted. I had never wanted to bring so much pain to the person I loved the most, but I just could not quit. I couldn't stop, I wouldn't stop. I looked Lumi deep in the eyes all the way to the soul. I wanted to say what Lumi wanted to hear, instead all I could say was, "I am sorry Lumi, I love you, but I can't stop."

The words visibly broke my Lumi, along with my heart. Lumi turned and left the apartment. I was left there on my own, not knowing what to feel. I found my way back to the couch and sat there, listening to the storm outside rage just like the one going on inside of me.

CHILLY RECEPTION

I woke up the next morning to the close rumbling of thunder and car alarms going off outside. The lake system was still pouring down on the city. As I looked out the window, the once busy blue streets were now empty, and back to their normal pavement grey. Just a few cars traversed the inundated road, splashing puddles into the air as they ran them over.

It would soon be time to head back and I had failed in erasing Mr. Michelson. I headed to the kitchen, leaving the window and the storm. I riffled through the fridge and cupboards. I ended up hunched over an overfilled bowl of cereal and my thoughts. I brushed last night's incident with Lumi aside and focused on how I could still erase Mr. Michelson in the little time I had left. It was 7:32 AM and I had maybe five, maybe six hours left here. I knew I had to be present at the "polar plunge" celebration, but otherwise the rest of the time was mine.

I picked up my phone and dialed Mr. Michelson's number. It was early, but he had to be on his way to work by now. The phone rang four times and eventually Mr. Michelson's normal voice broke through the phone.

"This is Patrick," he sounded cheery yet professional. I could hear the other voices in the background, one of them a child. He was still home; he was probably nervous and edgy from my call. I considered playing with him on the phone, but I decided against it. I knew he preferred the "hard to get" kind, but I was out of time, so I got right down to business.

"Hi Patrick, I hear this might not be the most opportune time, but I am incredibly upset and disappointed about last night."

"Yes, I know that was such a loss, what can I do to make it up to you Rob?" He had done this before and was keeping his cool in front of his family.

"Well I don't know who Rob is, but you can make it up to me during lunch today."

"Sure, that will work buddy, what were you thinking of specifically though?" His voice got calmer and calmer with every word he said. It made me want to erase him even more.

"You will come to my place, say noon, and have me for lunch." I gave him the address, he agreed and I hung up. I was going to be cutting it close, but I should be able to pull it off. I did get a little sad, I had grown to love the building, and I was going to have to burn it down along with Mr. Michelson.

The lake water was frigid, the constant drizzle of cold rain didn't offer any relief. I made it to the Polar Plunge celebration and reluctantly participated. I was immune to all diseases known to man, but cold was cold and no genetic alteration could help me escape it.

The mass of people had stripped down to swimsuits and pieces of clothing they were trying to pass off as swimsuits. After much debate, I had decided to wear a one piece female swimsuit. For some reason I had always seen myself as the dame and Lumi as my knight. The old man wearing a speedo which was hiding under his belly, started the countdown. Soon everyone joined in. We were all facing the dancing lake waters and being drenched by the cold rain. The crowd buzzed with anticipation and the voiced reached a crescendo as the countdown terminated. "3, 2, 1….."-- then a roar of screams, hoots and hollers. The sand shook and flew up in the air as we rushed the waters. There were maybe two thousands of us, but it truly sounded like a stampede of buffalos. Water joined the flying sand as the first wave of humanity reached the freezing water.

The screaming increased in quantity and pitch. The first droplet of airborne lake hit my face as I followed the crowd in the insane celebration. After a few more steps my feet got the frozen welcome of the water. Adrenaline kicked in and I kept on forward. Every step, the water kept creeping up my body and started to squeeze yelps out of me. Once the water was up to my chest, the wave of humanity stopped and we all splashed around in the cold water. Little by little, the crowd joined and before I knew it, everyone was singing "Go Cubs, Go!" while in the water. The choir of voices thundered through the misting rain and the smiles of the people lit the occasion like lightning in the night. I found myself overtaken by the moment, singing along and smiling like everyone else.

Once the song was done, the order was given and we slowly exited the chilly water. The short comfort I had found submerging in the water, evaporated once the air hit my body. Everyone, including me, was shaking and screaming once more. We huddled like penguins in the Artic until everyone was back out on the sand. The old man wearing the inappropriate speedo spoke once more. His voice still echoed through the crowd, but held an edge of trembling now. Once he was done, everyone seemed to scream at the top of their lungs and disperse in the search of dry, warm towels.

I found my bag and little pile of clothes, dried off, and headed back to the apartment. Mr. Michelson would be showing up soon and I wanted to be radiantly ready for him. The walk back was a miserable one. The swimsuit, even after my best efforts was still wet and the rain had turned from a mist to large cold droplets. I didn't have an umbrella so I resigned myself to being cold in the early November rain and walking fast.

I couldn't make it to the shower fast enough once back in the dry safety of the apartment. I turned the water as hot as I could tolerate and marinated in it. The warmth first burned, but as my body adjusted, it felt like the safety of the womb I had never experienced. I stopped myself from thinking and just felt the water hit my head and neck, sliding down my body making my skin goose bumps under its warm embrace.

My trance of relaxation was interrupted by the doorbell. Mr. Michelson had arrived as instructed. I debated how to greet him at the door. I finally settled on the classic girl towel around the torso. It would definitely help seduce him and communicate without a doubt what my intentions were. I wrapped the towel around my body and began my walk to the door. The doorbell rang once more and I made sure I was in full character for Mr. Michelson. He didn't know it, but he was in a rush to his own demise. I made it to the door, leaving a trail of water droplets behind me, and reached for the doorknob.

As I started to open the door I was flung across the room, while blinded by a bright flash. I caught myself and broke the fall as I hit the hardwood floor. I scrambled now, naked and seeking refuge behind the couch. I peeked around and what once was a door, was now slowly raining down to the apartment floor as ash. A figure stood just outside the doorway, somehow being perfectly hidden by the shadows of the hallway.

I didn't have to guess or deduce who it might be. I felt it in my core, it was the Auditor. I considered fighting for a second, but quickly came to my senses. My only option was to run. Behind me was one of the windows of what once had been my refuge apartment. I was naked and still a little dazed, but had no other options. I gathered myself and started my mad dash to the closed window. I could hear some sort of weapon discharging behind me. The sound was like a snake hissing followed by the ever approaching crackle of electricity. I ducked as the crackling ball of energy approached me from behind. I saw it fly by. It was a round sphere of bright light with miniature lightning bolts running throughout it. I saw it impact the wall and grow. I directed my eyes back to the window as the sphere left a 2 meter round hole on the wall.

The prospect of now having to lunge myself through glass, convinced me to change my path to the freshly open wound on the building's shell. I picked up the pace and quickly jumped through the new opening and out into the midday deluge. The rain drops started beating on my body as I rushed down to earth from the third story. I prepared myself for the landing and tried to figure out how I was going to remain inconspicuous, while naked, and surviving a three story fall in the middle of lunch hour rush. The streets below were littered with a mushroom field of umbrellas. At least not many, if any, would see me fall. I would more or less appear to them as a naked genital-less angel that fell from heaven during the rainstorm.

As I hit the pavement, rolled, and stood naked in the cold rain, I realized that keeping my true existence a secret was pretty irrelevant now. My dark hunter stood at the opening looking down upon me. I knew the Auditor would not open fire while I stood surrounded by innocent people. I also knew that any life I had known was now over. Lumi had tried to warn me and help me. I had been too stubborn to listen. Now I stood naked, cold, and completely cut off from everything I ever knew. I still had my wrist controls, but trying to jump to any other time would be foolish right now. I started running down the street, no longer holding back and running at my full speed. By the time any pedestrian realized they saw me, I would have been long gone.

My first priority was to find clothes and somewhere to hide out for a bit. I ran and I ran, before I knew it I was standing in front of The Sea Urchin. I didn't know what had guided me there, but the neon sign shone above me. I entered and Mike's usual head nod of a welcome was replaced by big surprised eyes. The Urchin was empty, but for one drunk hanging onto the bar in his drunken stupor. Mike came around from behind the bar and for the first time I heard him talk.

"What happened to you, kid?" He looked me up and down. I was pleased when he didn't linger on any of my body parts. "Come in, come in. Let's go to my office and see if I can find you something to wear."

I smiled and nodded as I held myself for warmth. He led me to a door that sat behind the bar and flanked the expensive bottles he would rarely use. He pressed his hand to a black pad. A light scanned his hand and the door unlocked. He opened it and ushered me in. I was surprised by the degree of technology for a place like this, but I guess Mike liked to be safe.

The room that lived on the other side of the door, looked, felt and more importantly, smelled nothing like the bar. It wasn't much of an office really. It did have a desk, a very nice wooden desk. It looked heavy, old and well cared for. On it was a single lamp, the old school type with the green covering and single bulb in it. The rest of what must have been his quarters were just as well taken care off and classy. There was a bed, a couple of brown leather chairs, a small table, a recliner and a small television in the corner. This must be where Mike lived. The extra expense on the security system made complete sense now.

"Please sit down." He pointed to one of the two wooden chairs at the table. "I am going to see if I can find you something to wear." He opened a pair of doors and his closet appeared within it. He started riffling through the hangers and scavenging through the boxes in the closet floor. After a few moments he turned with a few articles for me to try. He pointed to another door which led to the bathroom. I took the clothing from his hands and hurried in through the door.

The bathroom was all in marble and stone. It was classy and beautiful. It felt more like a spa than a bathroom and it even had the whirlpool tub to go with the spa feel. I closed the door and carried the pile of clothes Mike had given me over to the sink counter. The stonework was seamless and expensive. I looked at myself in the full wall mirror and I looked like shit. My hair was wet, I looked tired, and I could see the desperation in my eyes. I broke the stare with my disheveled self and started to look through the pile of clothes. I settled on a pair of sweatpants I could hold up with the draw string, along with a Cubs jersey. It didn't fit perfectly, but it would make do.

I washed my face and composed myself. I prepared to walk out and hesitated when reaching for the doorknob. My hand reached for it then went back down next to my body. I stood there paralyzed and horrified of what might be on the other side of that door. I looked behind me and there was no window to escape through. I closed my eyes and took a few deep breaths to calm myself down. When I reopened the door, it didn't explode, it just stood quietly in front of me. I considered putting my ear to the door to discover what might be hiding behind it, but opted against it. I filled myself with valor and reached for the doorknob and turned it. Nothing happened, the door sat quietly and the cold doorknob was still inside my grasp.

I opened the door and Mike's living quarters were just as I had left them. Mike sat at the small wooden table, his eyes instantly meeting me as I walked out. I approached him and he stood.

"Glad you found something that fit. I was starting to get worried there." He smiled and it was an honest and comforting smile. I felt myself smiling back at him. "Here I will take those from you." He grabbed the extra clothes from my hands and walked them back to his closet. He carefully put them away and joined me back by the table.

I was still standing where he had left me. "Please, please, sit down." He pointed toward the chair across from his. My mind was wandering elsewhere so I obeyed by reflex to his request. He excused himself and left me alone in the quiet studio as he disappeared through the door and back out into the bar. After a couple of quiet minutes, I heard the door click unlocked and he re-entered his home. He was carrying two water bottles and promptly handed me one as he sat. He opened his and took a sip. I mirrored him and drank half the bottle before I realized I was drinking it. I put the cap back on the bottle and set it on the dark wooden table.

"Thank you Mike, you didn't have to…." I stopped midsentence. "Thank you."

"Oh don't worry about it. You needed a helping hand. You would have done the same for me." His body language was much more relaxed from what I had seen in the bar and his hands talked as much as his mouth. "May I ask what happened?"

I considered how to answer him. He had been kind and deserved the truth. On the other hand he might think I was completely crazy if I told him the truth. I settled on; "You would not believe me if I told you, Mike. And by the way, I am Jordan."

He smiled and instantly extended his hand out to properly greet me. "Pleasure to officially meet you, Jordan," he said as he shook my hand. Once the pleasantries were finished, he surprised me by what he said. "I can tell you are not from around here, Jordan, and I am not talking a foreigner. I see and deal with those every day. So why don't you try me with the truth? I might believe more than what you think."

He finished talking and sat there with a friendly smile and inviting eyes. The man had probably saved my life, so against my better judgment I told him. This might be my last chance to share with someone what I had been doing all these years. If the Auditor was going to erase me, I was going to make sure my cause lived on.

I told Mike about my timeline, where I came from, what I did, and what was happening. He sat there the whole time listening and nodding to my every word. His eyes never glazed over and although he furrowed his brow a few times, he seemed to be following my fantastical tale. I didn't hold back a bit, even told him about my experiences with the Randoms and everything I had done to change my present. His face never showed any signs of disgust, so either he believed and agreed with me, or he thought I was mental. Either way he kept a calm, open and kind demeanor. Once I was done, I sat there in silence letting him process, and waiting the million questions I was expecting him to ask me.

"Well, it sounds like you are quite in a jam, Jordan. Wished I could help you more, but all I got to offer are the clothes and maybe a place for you to hide for a while." Mike broke the silence and surprised me with his remarks. Not a single question was asked. He didn't question the veracity of my story, he simply tried to help, and took me for my word. I was both glad and worried. Maybe he would snap later once it all had sunken in, or he had heard even more outrageous stories from his patrons. I decided to take his offer and kindness for the time being. Once he was sure I was settled in, he disappeared back out into the bar and left me to rest.

I didn't do much resting. I had deactivated my wrist unit, but half expected the Auditor to blast the door at any second. Mike's security system would prove no match for an energy blast if the Auditor did find me. The torturous thought that my goal had been thwarted broke my heart. I analyzed every moment of this scouting mission trying to figure out how I was found out. For the life of me, I could not understand how they figured it out, but somewhere I must have slipped. I was finally seeing my work pay some dividends and got sloppy. I had no one to blame but me for this. My mind kept jumping from memory to memory, over to what my plan of action was going to be, and my heart sobbed knowing I would never see Lumi again. Tears ran down my face as I lay on Mike's bed and before I realized it, darkness overtook me.

I woke up with Mike hovering over me. He was just staring and studying me. Luckily he kept a safe distance, because I jumped out of the bed ready to fight. I stopped myself inches from striking poor curious Mike. His eyes were the only thing that could react to my speed and they were wide as saucers as I stopped my fist inches from his face. I lowered my arms and stood there letting Mike absorb what just happened. His eyebrows arched up and he whistled an amazed sound. He backed away from me and found some refuge on one of the chairs by the table. I slowly approached him and sat across from him once more.

"I'm sorry Mike, I got startled. Are you ok?"

"I'm fine, I've just never seen anyone move so fast ever in my life. You were not kidding about the genetic modifications." He smiled as he shook his head to show me he was ok.

I knew I had scared him and might lose my temporary sanctuary because of it. There wasn't anything I could do to set him more at ease. I sat there and hoped he hadn't changed his mind about me.

"I am sorry to tell you I am not the Auditor, just a lowly bartender from the twenty-first century." His smile reassured me of my sanctuary. Finally the questions started to come out. He was very interested in my time with the Randoms. I shared everything I remembered from my time there. Yet his questions didn't end.

I was in the middle of explaining to him the reason for the buildings being round when we heard a large noise coming from behind the locked door. Mike had closed the bar for the night, so unless a drunk had stumbled out of the bathroom, I was in deep shit. He got up and went to what I thought was another closet in the wall. When he opened the double doors, a myriad of small TV monitors came to life. He eyes started to jump from one monitor to the next until he froze. He looked back at me then back to the monitor.

Whatever he had seen had changed his face to a grave expression. I didn't have to ask him what it was. I knew the Auditor had somehow found me and now I was a fish in a barrel to be hunted. Mike's concerned eyes once more rested upon me.

"You have to go, your friend is here." Even though his eyes looked panicked his voice remained the same cool, calm, and relaxed tone I had always heard.

"Unless you have a secret exit Mike, I am kind of stuck here."

"Come this way, Jordan." His feet moved with urgency and he headed for the bathroom. I quickly stood up and followed him. He headed for the shower, opened the door, and stepped in. He proceeded to push random tiles in a specific order and what was once the wall of the shower became an exit. "I have accumulated my fair share of enemies throughout the years, never hurts to be ready." He urged me to head through, giving me instructions on how to exit to the back ally.

Another explosion and loud noise stopped Mike from his instructions. The door to the living quarters had clearly been blown to toothpicks. I started to head down the secret corridor towards safety, but Mike didn't follow along. I stopped and urged him to move, but he remained still. I walked back towards the shower and Mike. The opening started to close and I started running towards it.

"You are not the only one," Mike said with his kind blue eyes as the opening shut before I could reach it. I tried to listen through the wall, but no noise came through. I did the only thing I could do and started heading down the hallway and to safety. As I spilled out in the early morning sun I asked myself what Mike meant. How was I not the only one? The only one what? I pushed the questions aside for another time and ran. I didn't have a plan nor knew where I was heading, but I ran as fast as I possibly could, away from the Auditor.

EMERGENCY EXIT

I found myself in front of the lake, the waves gently lapping at the shore. It was cold and the rain had turned to wet slushy snow. There was not another soul as far as the eye could see, just me, the lake and the city pressing behind me. I knew it was only a matter of time before the Auditor found me. I had nowhere and everywhere to go. The strings of time stretched out in front of me like the endless lake. Unfortunately every time I traveled, the Auditor would know, and bring his wrath along. I considered getting lost in the eons of time, I contemplated staying and fighting, eventually I settled on searching for the help of the people I was trying to become.

I set my arm unit for my time, but a different location than KronoCorp. I knew the village of the Randoms where poor Lucy had been slain was nothing but ashes now. I did remember the village of Lake Umatilla where her son had moved to, I set my coordinates as close to it as I could and off I went.

I came to on my knees, throwing up every ounce of bile I had in my stomach. Without the dampers at KronoCorp, the ride had been extremely turbulent. I convulsed and my body spasmed, tears ran out of my eyes and I gasped for air. Through the tears and panic I could see a different lake stretch out in front of me. Instead of the grey of the city, I was surrounded by different shades of green and warm browns. I saw a figure approaching me and for a moment I saw Lucy. As my eyes cleared and I regained control of my organs, I realized it was a young woman. I was smiling at the specter of what I thought was my old friend. The flesh and blood girl smiled back at me, her hair as blazing red as Lucy's had been. I tried to talk, but my lungs were still trying to figure out how to work.

The girl kept approaching and was now kneeling next to me. Her hand started to caress my back in a circular motion. The sensation of her hand on me was both overwhelming and comforting. My muscles started to slowly relax under her touch, allowing me to slowly function once more. My eyes finished focusing and I could see I was in a pine forest facing out onto the lake. I could feel the dead pine needles under my hands mixed with the dirt. My nose picked up the scent of flowers and I turned my head realizing the spectacular aroma was emanating from the girl kneeling next to me. I tried to talk once more and this time the circuits worked.

"I need to see Michael, son of Lucy." The girl's hand stopped rubbing my back and she got up to her feet. She extended her hand to me, as if to help me up. I looked at it for a few moments and slowly reached for it. With much of her help, I found myself standing next to her. I tried walking and almost fell, apparently not all circuits were back to normal yet. She put her arm around my waist and I put mine over her shoulder. She helped me through a path in the forest. With every step I slowly remembered how to control my body. Eventually, I was able to let go of the beautiful and aromatic girl as we walked. Ahead, I started to see the familiar circular structures. Once more I was greeted with the friendly, but worried faces I had seen at Lucy's village. The girl would wave and the villagers would go back to where they were going.

We weaved our way through the circular log buildings until we started approaching what must have been their town hall. The girl ushered me in and guided me towards a back table where several Randoms were gathered in serious conversation. The voices were hushed, but held a palpable intensity.

We finally reached the table where thirteen people sat, each one of them so different from the next. Skin tones as dark as the night, to white like clouds and everything in between, eyes in all shapes and colors, heads adorned with a multitude of hair color, even one smooth and shiny scalp. I envied them, so different and so beautiful.

"Michael, someone is here to see you." The girl broke them out of their intense conversation. The concerned and passionate expressions evaporated, leaving 12 pairs of eyes fixated on me. The man with his back to us stood and slowly turned to greet us. His hair was dark brown and had broad strong shoulders. As he turned, I slowly began to recognize the man who stood before me. The nose, the mouth, the kind and inviting eyes were all too familiar to me. I soaked it all in and waited for him to talk. He was younger than when I had first met him, but undoubtedly was one in the same.

Mike stood in front of me, the same kind eyes, the same soft smile, just younger. "Happy to see you Jordan, didn't expect you this soon, but glad to see you none the less." I stood paralyzed as the words escaped his lips.

"Please sit, we must talk." An empty chair had appeared next to me and room had been made at the table. Without a word I sat down and

PRIME INFINITY

wondered what kind of trap I had walked myself into.

Once more I looked at all the faces attentively staring at me. They slowly started to become familiar. They were not strangers at a Random's village, but faces I had seen during my scouting missions. How was that possible? I wasn't dead yet, so that was a good sign. I sat and waited for the prying eyes to become words that explained what was going on.

"I see you recognize some of us. I assure you, this is a safe place for you, Jordan." Mike's voice was as reassuring and caring as I remembered. I thought all the warnings about messing with the timeline were bullshit. But I had proof sitting in front of me to the contrary. I kept looking at the faces around me and more of them became familiar. An older woman, about as old as Lucy should have been by now, broke the silence.

"Your visit to the redwoods village was a very memorable one in our history, Jordan." My eyes now fixated on her, she gently smiled and introduced herself. "My name is Abemi, I am one of the elders of this village, and am very familiar with you." Her skin was dark and silky. Her ebony head had the most delectable shine to it. Her eyes were intense white orbs with vibrant brown pupils. Her hair was white and kept very short, close to her scalp. As she continued to talk, her voice was deep and rich and I could feel her words dance around while caressing my skin. All the eyes penetrated into my soul as Abemi continued with her tale.

"I know you knew Lucy, I would be considered her counterpart in our village. I have heard of that ugly day, we have all heard of it. Unlike what everyone thought, a few survivors got away, three to be exact. Each of them decided to head to a different village and spread the news about what had happened, and the news of Jordan's visit."

She remained neutral as she spoke, but my visit had brought nothing but doom to the redwoods village. I was worried I was going to be made to pay for what happened. As if reading my mind she continued.

"Ever since Red Wednesday, we have been keeping an eye on you, Jordan. At first our motives were to find possible guilt in your actions and figure out how to kill you." I swallowed hard at her words. "But once we saw what you were and what you were doing, we changed our objectives. Your mission has been a very noble one and we support it. We have followed you along now for the past five years in your endeavors. Most of the time we just observed, but every once in a while, we interceded to help you."

That was more to swallow than I had expected. My solitude had been my resolve and strength in what I was doing. It was me against, not only the world, but time as well. I found comfort and strength in walking the hard path on my own. Now undeniably, by the look of the surrounding faces, that had never truly been the case. These Randoms had watched, helped, and protected me all along. I didn't know whether to feel grateful or angry.

"I believe you, I recognize your faces, but how could you have possibly followed me all these years? I mean you guys don't even have the technology!" My tone was harsh, even to me, as anger spilled over into my words. I gathered myself, but didn't apologize.

"We choose this life, Jordan." Her long strong arms extended out as to present me the great hall. "But we are not naïve, nor strangers to the technologies of the world." She sat there, her piercing brown eyes pressing on me, letting me absorb and process what she had truly said.

"How did you obtain the technology?" Her smile widened, recognizing my understanding.

"You are not the only member of Civilization which found discontent in their perfect lives. Throughout the decades, relationships were forged. Information and technology were leaked out to us. We refused to incorporate it into our everyday life, but will use it in extreme cases. You, Jordan, are an extreme case."

"What makes me so special? If it weren't for me, redwoods village would be safe and sound." Anger once more got away from me. I didn't like feeling like a puppet and spitefully dug at them. A few bodies shifted and tensed at my words, but calm prevailed as Abemi continued.

"You aren't special." The words stung and surprised me. "But you have gotten further than anyone before you. Maybe the time is right, maybe you are lucky or maybe you are a little special. Whichever the case, Jordan, the fact is that you have made great strides and we want to see it to completion."

A short white man approached me, coming over from another table at Abemi's signal. I recoiled at first, as he invaded my space, but Abemi explained. "This is Jack, he is one of our techs and will help modify your arm controller. Please forgive him; he is not much of a people person, but a genius with machines."

I refused to give Jack access to my arm controller. Even if we were on the same side, I was not giving up my only way to escape this place. I knew the Auditor would track me down, I had to be ready to escape.

Noticing my apprehension, Abemi chimed in. "Jack is only going to make it harder for the Auditor to find you." Her knowledge of the Auditor distracted and hypnotized me. Questions started to flood into my brain and by the time I had realized my mental paralysis, Jack was well into my arm controller. I gave in and let him do what he needed to do.

After about five minutes of pressing buttons, poking at the controller and shocking me a few times with feedback, Jack was done. Without a word, he gave Abemi a look to let her know he was done. I sat there caressing the skin around the arm controller trying to massage away the still lingering tingle of the electric shocks.

"Your main and back-up locators have been disabled. This will make you much harder to track. Your DNA locator is impossible to disrupt so it means it won't be impossible to find you, just very difficult. All your travel will be independent, so hopefully you either get used to it, or get used to throwing up. Now let's go, we must send you off on your way."

"Send me off?" Why would they go through all the trouble of hiding me just to get rid of me?

"Yes, like I said difficult, but not impossible. We cannot run the risk of you staying here. Don't worry. Martina has already come up with your first rabbit hole jump." Abemi stood and motioned me towards the exit. We left the large room and I followed her through the maze of buildings. We finally stopped at the door of a small round wooden building on the outskirts of the village. I could feel the buzz of the village behind me, while I could see the infinity of the forest ahead of us. Abemi knocked on the door, the door opened and a beautiful blonde vision stood in front of us.

She was shorter than me, but what little clothes she wore clung to a sea of curves. She was voluptuous, sensuous, and everything that a woman should be. As beautiful as I was, I was nothing compared to her raw beauty. Her white tank top hung from her shoulders, navigated down through her supple breasts and finished right above her exposed flat stomach and friendly belly button. She wore brown fabric pants like most of the villagers I had seen. Well what was left of them, they left her strong legs exposed and tempted the eye of more private things.

By the time I was done soaking in every inch of Martina, Abemi had disappeared. Martina smiled at me. "Come on in!" Her voice sounded as succulent and velvety as her tanned skin must have felt.

I looked back once more in search of what I thought was my guide, but Abemi was lost in the village behind me. I entered the small structure and felt as if I had walked back into KronoCorp. The wooden exterior of the small building hid a plethora of technology within in.

"I can't believe I am in front of the infamous Jordan." Martina's childlike excitement grabbed my attention and made me smile.

"I'm Martina." Her hand extended out to me. Her emerald green eyes were a little too wide with excitement and her blonde ponytail seemed to dance as her body vibrated. I took her soft and gentle hand and shook it. Her skin felt every bit as soft and delicate as I had imagined. My nose finally caught up with the rest of my senses and it just added to her luscious allure. She smelled of the morning dew and blooming flowers under the sun. My senses overtook me and it was poor Martina who was forced to break the overfriendly handshake.

She shook off the momentary awkwardness, turned her back to me, and started talking as she approached one of the consoles. "Here is what I figured. You will do a quad jump. The first three will help keep them off your scent. The fourth and last jump will be your temporary refuge."

"How long will this "quad jump" keep them off my trail?" Her face was instantly somber as I asked my question, giving me an uncomfortable feeling in the depths of my entrails.

"Well, if everything works well, a week per jump." The way Martina pushed the words out from behind a forced smile told me there was more to that statement.

"And if they don't?" My eyes no longer hypnotized by her beauty, urged her to answer.

She broke my intense gaze and readied to answer. "If they can trace your DNA signal quickly, you have at most a day per jump."

I had either a month or four days until I was found. Talk about living looking over your shoulder. "What if I do more than four jumps?"

Once more her beautiful face worried at my inquiry. "Four is the limit you can do in row before your system shuts down." She stood there trying to look as inoffensive and cute as possible after the words left her lips.

System shuts down; what a mechanically and poetic way to tell me I might keel over and die. "How long do I have to wait before I can jump again, without dying?"

Her expression kept evolving from worried to grim with every one of my questions. "You have to wait at least two weeks before you can jump again. The arm control draws too much energy from your cells. If you don't allow your body to heal between repeated jumps, the micro nuclear reactions will destabilize your molecular structure to the point you won't be able to heal."

"So I have four days for certain, but have to wait two weeks to jump again. What am I supposed to do during the other ten days, Martina?"

Her response was all too quick. "Simple, just be you." The childlike smile returned to her face and she beamed with more confidence in me than I had in myself. I wasn't sure what she thought I was, or who I really was, but the adoration in her eyes gave me hope for myself.

"I have chosen the first three destinations for you. I have picked them for their population density and genetic composition. It should make tracking you much more difficult. The last destination you are to pick and enter yourself, once you have arrived at the third. After the two weeks have lapsed you can do another quad jump. I am to instruct you not to return here in your jumps until you have successfully completed three quad jumps. And please, for the safety of us all, never make this your final jump."

I listened very carefully to the very intelligent and beautiful blonde. Once she was done with all her instructions and warning we went over the destinations she had picked for me. First I was to jump to Vatican City during the conclave that elected Pope Francis in 2,013. After that I was to jump to global peace talks of 3,395. The final jump was to be the most dangerous. Back 60,000 years to the origins of homo sapiens and the genetic pool.

Martina carefully walked me through the directions to input the last location once I had reached the prehistoric age. She warned me of all the dangers of each jump and reassured me that Jack's modification should dampen the effects of the trips.

After all the warnings had been relayed to me from her soft lips, she checked the time and instructed me it was time to go. I still had many questions for her, for Abemi, and Michael. The urgency in her eyes told me my questions would have to wait. Her body vibrated and jumped until she could not resist herself anymore. She lunged forward and embraced me in a hug. It was tender and intense. Her body pressed against mine made imaginary parts of me long for her. Once the tight hug broke, the look of pure admiration in her vibrant green eyes gave me the courage and determination for what I was about to do.

All goodbyes said, I turned my attention to the control panel on my arm. I looked back and forth several times between the control panel and Martina. She was patient with me, but I knew I had to just plunge and go for it. I pressed the last command and off I went.

HIDE AND SEEK

Every jump was more fascinating than the last. I wanted to stop, explore, and scout the events and locations. As great as the temptation was, I reminded myself of Martina's instructions. For the quad jump to work properly, I only had 139 seconds. So with great regret I would give my surrounding one good look and proceed to the next jump.

By the time I landed in prehistory, Jack's modifications were reaching their limitations. I had to concentrate hard not to leave my stomach contents and genetic material all over the savannas of Africa. Once I had composed myself and taken my peek around, I proceeded to enter the coordinates for my temporary hiding spot.

I had considered it carefully while talking with Martina, and with every jump I had grown more convinced on where I should go. I looked at the timer on the arm controls and it read 128 seconds. I had let my curiosity wander too much with each jump and now I had very little time to enter both the geographical and temporal coordinates while feeling nauseous and dizzy.

The panic in my gut triggered a surge of adrenaline and I furiously entered the commands into the small console on my forearm. The unforgiving timer kept ticking upwards towards 139 seconds as my fingers flew over the commands. 136, 137, 138, I struggled to enter the last coordinates. I hit the travel command as the timer turned to 139, I closed my eyes and hoped I wasn't too late.

I found myself on my knees throwing up every ounce I had managed to hold back just a few seconds ago. I let my body spasm and get everything out of it needed, instead of fighting to hold it in. It helped. I kept my eyes closed through the whole visceral experience. Even after my body had stopped fighting my will, I remained on my hands and knees with my eyes closed. Fear kept them closed for me. Had I made the final jump? Was I now stuck in prehistory for two weeks?

Neither option was too promising really, so I kept my eyes closed. While they remained closed I could escape the desperate reality which my life had become. My ears betrayed me. The gentle lapping of the waves on the sandy shore told me where I was. Unable to escape from myself, I chose to remain there and just enjoy the relaxing sound of the water. I could hear the seagulls in the distance and the aquatic trance was broken. I opened my eyes and found my fingers clenched and dug into the sand. I reminded myself to breath and took a lungful of cold air into my chest.

I slowly raised my head, my eyes tracing the sandy shore all the way up to the embankment. I could see the gray city off in the distance, a chilling and cold sanctuary. I gathered myself to my feet, wiping the sand off my hands and knees. The universe had stopped spinning in my head and I was finally able to focus. The city loomed ahead, just a day ahead of where I had left it. This would be the last place they would expect me to come and hide. Plus, I had a little unresolved business with Mr. Michelson. I remembered Martina's eyes, filled myself with their courage, and placed one foot in front of the other. I headed into the city ready to face my future and to end Mr. Michelson's.

Waves of nausea and dizziness would slow me and make the city blur on me. My resolve remained strong and I fought through the everlasting waves of discomfort as I approached the looming city. I walked for what seemed a couple of hours until I finally decided where to go. The apartment, The Sea Urchin, and anywhere that was once safe was now off limits. I was pretty sure the Auditor was no longer around, but I did not want to run the risk. I headed to the tall business building that provided Mr. Michelson shelter during the day.

I hid behind a newspaper and sat in the lobby as I had once before. I kept my eyes peeled, but my mind wandered and missed Lumi. My stomach ached and it wasn't from hunger. It was the need and longing that overwhelmed me. I had pushed it aside, but I was worried sick about my Lumi. I knew Lumi could handle most things, but this was the Auditor we were talking about. I also pondered on how involved Lumi was. Is that where the technology and information came from? Who else was helping? Had Lumi been found out?

Unanswerable questions haunted me for the next few hours as I pretended to read the ancient information carrier. Finally, Mr. Michelson's fancy suit broke me out of my melancholic trip. I had to hurry up and follow him as he darted out of the lobby. He seemed concerned and was moving with a purpose. I was careful to tail him while remaining undetected. He kept looking at his expensive gold watch as he pounded the pavement through the cold city. He stopped darting through the sidewalks and started to make his way up the simple steps that led to a lavish church.

Mr. Michelson disappeared through the doors of the church and I felt reluctant to follow. I found a good watching post and settled in to wait for him to exit.

Not much time passed and he reappeared at the door. An older woman wearing her full nun habit was smiling and conversing with him. Even from a distance, I could tell Mr. Michelson was apologizing to the patient nun. They said their goodbyes and Mr. Michelson started to make his way down the steps with his young son in hand. They held each other's hands as they walked and conversed with each other. The young boy was wearing a shirt and pants which looked like a uniform, under his open blue coat. The child would walk, jump, and skip down the steps as his dad held on to his hand and provided him safety.

Even at his young age, the kid looked just like Mr. Michelson. It was like watching a young and older version of the same person walk down those steps. The hunter and the killer were nowhere to be found in Mr. Michelson's face. He had the same content and happy smile he had when I had seen him at the parade with his family. The monster and the younger version of him walked down the sidewalk and I kept following. The young child seemingly had a lot to tell his father, for I didn't see his mouth stop for more than a few seconds. His father would nod and listen and guided them through the foot traffic on the sidewalks.

At last they made it to an apartment building and sought shelter from the cold inside. The door man greeted both the small and the large Mr. Michelson's and opened the door for them. I recognized the place as his home, but I had never seen him bring the child there with him. Tired of being out in the cold, I found a pizzeria across the street and settled in for an early dinner.

The lady at the front took my order and explained to me it would take 30-40 minutes to get my pizza. Being that this might be my last meal, I decided to go for the gusto. I stacked the pizza with as many toppings as I could, ordered some appetizers, and a drink. I requested a table by the front window and was seated after waiting for a couple of minutes. Once the nice young lady had showed me to my table, she disappeared back into the rumble of the restaurant, weaving her way in between the narrow spaces between the tables.

I watched the street as I sipped on my over sugared soda. Slowly the fried morsels started to arrive at my table. The restaurant was starting to get busy with the dinner crowd. I blocked out as much of the happy workers as I could and savored every greasy bite. The sidewalks were much calmer than a few days before. I kept overanalyzing my encounter with Lumi as I was leading Mr. Michelson to his last breaths. Lumi knew something but could not tell me, that must have been awful. I wished we could talk about it, but I knew Lumi had to keep cover also.

The waitress delivered to my table a round disk about two inches high and nine inches across. The outer edge of the disk was a golden yellow and surrounded a slightly smaller red disk inside of it. The smell intensified as she placed the delicious disk on the table. She proceeded to cut out a triangular slice out of the orb and placed it in a small plate in front of me. As she dislodged the triangular slice the strings of white held on to the mother disk, but to no avail. I could see all the toppings I had indulged in, in my beautiful slice of deep dish pizza. She asked if I needed anything else and left me to my delicacy.

I savored every bite and when the poor girl came to ask if I needed a "to go" box, she was amazed to find the whole pizza pie gone. By now there was a line exiting the restaurant of hungry patrons trying to get in. The girl asked if I wanted anything else and I decided to reward myself with some tiramisu and wine.

I kept an eye out for Mr. Michelson as I relished each creamy bite of the decadent dessert. I had eaten enough to keep me for a few weeks, but Mr. Michelson hadn't shown his face on the streets yet. I started ordering wine, when I noticed the poor girl was getting anxious at my attachment with the table, I slipped her a couple of hundred dollar bills and her stress disappeared. She kept bringing me wine glasses and beers for the next three hours. The crowd was starting to thin down in the restaurant, when Mr. Michelson finally exited the apartment building. His body language and expression were back now to the more familiar predatory ones I had seen so much.

I quickly dropped a few more hundred dollar bills on the table, entered the cold night and followed Mr. Michelson on his latest escapade. I kept my distance as he confidently strode through the streets. Eventually, we arrived at a bar and not The Sea Urchin. I was a little disappointed not to be visiting our old stomping grounds, but I guess he had moved on to more fertile lands. The sign above the bar said "The Olive". Mr. Michelson entered; I waited a few minutes and entered the swanky place.

The crowd outside was littered with short black dresses and dress shirts. I had procured some clothing at a Laundromat on my walk back into the city, but felt incredibly underdressed. I hurried to find a secluded place so I could get out of sight. I might have only been wearing some tight jeans and a blouse, but I managed to get quite a few eager looks from some of the men in the bar.

I kept looking everywhere for Mr. Michelson, but he was nowhere in sight. The bar had plenty of dark spots; it was a swanky martini lounge. There was a long bar, expensive bottles of spirits proudly displayed and illuminated with blue lights. The bottles and the liquor inside of them took on a blue hue drawing your eyes towards them. The only thing to distract the eye away from the bottles, were the two bartenders sensually pouring drinks. The male bartender's torso was completely naked. His muscles rippling and contracting as he manhandled the bottles and martini shakers. The female matched him, but for what must be one of the smallest bikini tops I had ever seen. Her ample and obviously surgically enhanced breasts, had nothing more than a 2x2x2 triangle which hid where her nipples must have been. Otherwise, the strings holding the glorified pasties left nothing to the imagination. I was amazed how the small little blue triangles of fabric stayed put as she violently shook a martini while giving her entranced patron her most devilish smile.

Contrary to the long slick bar, with its half-naked bartenders, was a garden of plush leather couches. Creating micro private areas, all of them were illuminated just enough to still keep their secret charm. I found an open loveseat and made a bee line towards it. Mr. Michelson must have already found comfort in one of the poufy leather seats for I could not spot him. Once in my sheltered loveseat, a barely clothed waitress came over holding a round tray pinned between her arm and her torso and a small notebook at hand. She smiled and greeted me, making me welcome and somewhat uncomfortable with her outfit. Like the bartender, she wore a bikini top that barely did an adequate job at hiding the nipples on her overblown breasts. Her bottom was just as tiny, if not more scandalous. The matching blue bikini bottom had a small triangle in her precious area and strings holding it in place. Once the pleasantries were over and I had given her my order, she turned just to show that the small string continued around, disappearing between her plump butt cheeks. Her matching blue heels clicked and clacked as she walked my order back to the blue lit bar.

I pried my eyes away from the swaying hips show and went back to try to spot Mr. Michelson. I would have hated to follow him in here just to lose him. It wasn't until the scantily dressed waitress delivered some drinks to the corner booths that he did me the favor of sticking his face out into the light. He leaned forward to receive his drink and give the waitress his most inviting smile and cheesy line. She smiled and giggled as expected, but I caught her rolling her eyes as she walked away from the over excited Mr. Michelson.

Once the waitress was gone, he disappeared back into the shadows of his couch and continued to watch the crowd. Now I had spotted him, I was able to see him in the dimly lit corner. He did his usual scanning and hunting for prospective prey as I had seen him do at The Sea Urchin. His eyes started to chase the almost naked waitress as she left the bar with a martini glass filled with blue liquid carefully balanced on her small round tray. His eyes moved up and down the body of the young woman as she strutted through the bar. Eventually, the blue drink and almost naked waitress found their way to me. Mr. Michelson's eyes had followed the woman with lust and hunger, but once he saw me as the waitress handed me my drink, his face changed.

The predatory eyes he had been accosting the waitress with receded and a look of fear and panic overtook him. He swallowed down the liquor that danced in his mouth, set his drink down, and started to head towards the bathroom. He walked again with the hurried man on a mission walk from earlier. I had expected him to come join me after he had seen me, but instead he made a quick dash away from me. I knew something was not right, I gulped down my overpriced concoction, threw some money on the glass table, and went after him.

As I turned the corner down the hallway towards the bathroom, I saw the back exit door finish bouncing from a hasty exit. "Why was he running away from me?" I thought to myself. I hurried down the corridor and exited into the cold night. I could not see Mr. Michelson, but I could hear his running footsteps coming from my right. I left the ally and entered the street sidewalk. Mr. Michelson had made another right and was walking as fast as he could while fumbling his cell phone. He kept looking over his shoulder, back in my direction. He spotted me and picked up his pace. He was now moving somewhere between a trot and fast walk. He took one last look at me and redirected his attention back to his cell phone.

I made haste and stealthily caught up to him. I crossed the street and he kept his attention on his phone and a white card he was holding in his other hand. I could see him reading and dialing the numbers from the card into his phone. He looked back where he had expected me to be and not seeing me, he slowed down a bit. The phone in his hand went up to his ear and he waited. I could not make out completely what he said during his conversation, but I was able to make out the three words he repeated frantically into his phone.

"She is here, she is here, she is here," Mr. Michelson uttered loudly, and realizing the panic in his voice, he calmed his tone for the rest of his hushed conversation.

His panic transferred to me at the possibilities of who he could be calling. It was only day one of my jump and desperate thoughts started to cross my mind. I calmed the screams in my head and continued to follow Mr. Michelson. I had grown tired of his elusiveness and bullshit, so I decided it was time to act.

I stayed undetected as I followed him and with each step he seemed to relax a bit more. His eyes frantically searched the night for me, but were unable to spot me. Although he thought he had lost me, he was still wondering through the cold city streets in a random fashion. He really wasn't heading anywhere; he was just trying to make sure he lost me.

I played his game and chased carefully, waiting for my chance. As we headed further and further away from the nightlife, the foot traffic on the streets became thinner and thinner. I spotted a dark alley up ahead on Mr.

Michelson's side of the street. I figured it had to be now or never.

As Mr. Michelson approached the dark mouth of the alley, I prepared myself to quickly dash across the street. Once the moment was right, I moved as fast as I could towards Mr. Michelson. He didn't see me until the last second and by then we were both flying into the privacy of the alley as I tackled him like a freight train. He let out an airless protest as my shoulder dug into his ribs. The bones cracked and snapped in sharp wet sounds under his skin. I landed on top of him and as he tried to catch his breath, I pulled him further into the dark alley by his fancy pink shirt. He tried to protest as I drug him through the dirty pavement, but the noises were hushed and devoid of air.

I found even more seclusion behind a large green dumpster. I picked Mr. Michelson up by his shirt with one hand and tossed him against the wall. His eyes opened wide at the disbelief of my strength. Once his body was done traveling through the air, it made a large thudding sound as it hit the concrete wall. His feet caught him, but he slumped into the ground. Through the darkness, the fear filled the whites of his eyes and directed me towards him.

He watched as I approached him while crumpled on the ground. He tried to flee, but every time he moved shooting pain from his broken ribs paralyzed him. He could not get away, all he could do was watch my slow approach, and hold his ribs trying to breath. I finally closed the short distance and mounted his torso pinning his arms between my legs and his body. His eyes closed and his face protested at the shooting pain it caused him. He slowly opened his eyes while tears started to stream down the side of his face.

"Well hello Mr. Michelson, where were you heading so fast?" My voice was sexy, but it even sounded evil to me. His eyes widened and tears started to pool in the corner of his left eye by his nose. He tried to reply, but his lips only trembled. I slowly moved my hands towards his neck and small painful sobs started to exit out of his throat.

"This is how you like to kill your victims, isn't it? I watched you at the lake. I saw what you did to that poor girl. It is time for you to stop Mr. Michelson and I will make sure you do."

My hands tightened around his neck and he fought with what little he had left. His eyes narrowed and focused as he tried to free his arms from under me. The pool of tears kept growing on his left eye and with every move his broken ribs caused him to exhale in pain. My squeeze remained constant on his neck with both of my hands. First his arms stopped fighting as his mouth started to make small gasping noises in search of air. His eyes went from defiant to wide and accepting. I looked into Mr. Michelson's eyes and he stared right back at me as his brain slowly begun to shut down. The tears kept flowing out of him while his mouth opened desperately trying to find one gulp of air. The light in his eyes slowly faded away as his pupils slowly dilated completely open, allowing me to look deep into his tortured soul. Finally his lungs stopped struggling for air, his neck muscles relaxed, and the light in his eyes evaporated.

I held on for a few extra moments of anger, remembering the monster I had seen at the lake. The monster was now gone and empty eyes pooled with tears stared back through me and into infinity. I removed my hands from his lifeless neck and searched his pants for his cell phone. After a few tries I deciphered his password and unlocked his phone. I found the call log and redialed the last number he had called.

The phone began to ring and I anxiously waited for who might pick up on the other side. I was now standing in the dark alley and away from Mr. Michelson's now dead body. On the fourth ring I heard the line on the other side answer.

"Mr. Michelson, I told you I would call you as soon as I arrived. Go home and get away from her as I instructed you. Do you understand?" The voice was exasperated and angry at being bothered again. It also sent chills through my spine. I recognized the voice and knew exactly what it meant. My heart sank in my chest as I hung up the dead man's phone. I could hear the dreaded voice on the other side of the line repeating itself in an even more irritated tone as I hit the end call button on the screen. My four days of refuge had instantly disappeared. I had nowhere to go; they knew where I was, and were coming for me. I looked back at Mr. Michelson's shell and hated myself for having fallen into the trap.

HALLOW DRINKS

I walked away from the dark alley without a destination or direction. They knew where I was, it would just be a matter of time before they tracked me down. I walked and walked in the cold night hoping for inspiration for my next move. After a couple of hours of wandering, I found myself in front of the familiar and strange sign. It was dark now, its neon lights dead in the night's sky. I tried the front door and it was locked. I walked back around the alley and hoped I had better luck with the back door.

The alley was dark and ominous. The light of the street only penetrated so deep into the chilled concrete corridor. Deep in the shadows a single bulb illuminated the backdoor of The Sea Urchin. Subsequent lights deeper in the alley illuminated other doors, each one like a small buoy of light floating in the darkness. I stood at the mouth of the alley, the light calling me, while the darkness in between kept me at bay.

I stopped my stalling and left the security of the sidewalk. Soon I was walking in total darkness; my eyes adapted and prevented me from running into or tripping on anything. My pace quickened as I walked through the dark void. I was guided by the flickering bulb above The Sea Urchin's back door and although it was just a few meters, the walk felt like it took forever. I finally reached the safety of the light without anything jumping me and taking me forever into the darkness.

I went to turn the knob on the door, but it was gone. The door was propped closed and had a piece of lumber nailed to it and the door frame to keep it shut. I quickly pulled off the two by four, tossed it aside, and entered the familiar Urchin. The place was a complete mess. Mike's fight with the Auditor had left the place in shambles. I made my way out of the back hallway and into the main bar. There wasn't a single table or chair sitting or standing as they should. Most of them lay in pieces, scattered like giant toothpicks all over the floor.

The bar didn't fare much better. There were a couple of massive holes burned through the stout wooden bar. The holes exposed the secrets Mike kept hidden behind it. As I approached the bar, my shoes began to stick to the floor with each step, making a wet ripping sound with every step I took. The bar stools were all missing, all having joined the mess on the floor as pieces of shredded wood. I found the light switches as I made my way behind the bar and was only then truly able to soak in the total devastation the poor bar stood in.

My sticky footsteps turned into dangerous ones, as I walked through shards of broken bottles and mirrors behind the bar. Every bottle behind the bar lay on the ground broken, with their fermented entrails spilled all over the floor. All, except one. A single bottle of vodka remained strong and proud on the wall shelves behind the bar. I felt an instant kinship to it under my current circumstances, so I did the right thing and grabbed it. I knew it wouldn't have an effect on me, but the bottle deserved to be drunk.

I carefully tiptoed my way from the bottle massacre behind the bar and worked my way towards Mike's secured room. Well it was once secured; being that the door was completely missing it had lost some of its security. The room looked even worse than the bar. The furniture, the bed, everything but a chair and the small table, was broken and in shambles on the floor.

I weaved through the mess on the floor and took residence at the solitary chair and table. I put the unopened bottle of vodka on the table while I soaked in the mess I was in, and I didn't mean the bar. I opened the bottle of spirits, took a swig, and enjoyed the warm burn all the way to my stomach. I had grown to enjoy the sensation, it made me feel more human and alive somehow. I kept sipping on the bottle while thinking of the past, the future, and the present. I felt so tempted to jump again, but I was very certain I would not survive it. I drank and tried to decipher what my next move would be. Time was ticking and it was just an eventuality before they found me. Would it be worth it to fight? Or should I just keep running for the next 4 days?

I sat there in the darkness of the room. The lights from the bar shone through the busted doorway creating a misshapen rectangle of yellow, on the room's floor. With every sip I missed Lumi more and more. Before I knew it, I lifted the expensive vodka bottle and it was empty. I had lost track of time, which seemed very ironic for someone like me. I stood up to go throw the bottle away just to find myself stumbling, my equilibrium and eyes betraying me. This was an alien feeling and I could not help myself from giggling as I held onto the wall for balance. The bottle fell out of my hand making a crashing sound as it joined all the other broken bottles on the floor. My giggles turned into soft sobs, as all I wanted was to run to

Lumi. I wanted to share this experience, feel Lumi's skin, touch it, and taste it more than I had ever before. There was a burning in my loins I had never felt before and I ached for Lumi.

I was biting my lower lip as I stumbled back to the solitary chair. Once I ungracefully deposited myself into the chair, I felt a warmness overwhelm me. At first I thought it was my longing for Lumi, but soon realized the burning was coming from my stomach. I bent over in my chair and the contents of my stomach found their liberty through my mouth. The hot acid liquid burned my esophagus as it violently exited out of me. I gave in to it, relaxed and let it happen. I had fought back the contents of my stomach enough for one day, it was time they won.

Once empty I stood, tried to find my equilibrium, and went in the search of water. I was instantly parched and felt like my tongue had become sand paper. I found the metal coolers behind the bar and started opening door after door. Beer, beer and more beer is all I found. I considered drinking one, but my drunken meandering was rewarded by a couple of bottles of water buried in the corner of the cooler. I sucked down the first bottle and started to nurse the second. I was hunched over holding onto the bar when a noise came from the back door. It broke me out of my fabulous drunken experience and set all my senses on high alert.

I quickly snapped out of my temporary frozen state and ran towards the front door as fast as I could. The energy blasts started blasting behind me. Pieces of wood started raining down as each energy blast missed me and found the poor bar. I braced my shoulder and slammed through the front door. As soon as I exited into the streets, the blasts stopped and I knew my pursuer would be hot on my heels. I didn't hesitate, adrenaline quickly sobered me up and I ran as fast as I could away from The Sea Urchin.

I ran and ran, the buildings flashed by me on both sides. I wasn't sure which direction I was running in until Wrigley Field passed me on my left. I was running at my full potential, throwing caution to the wind. We were always warned to never use our abilities to their maximum, since it could be dangerous for our health. The least of my worries was blowing up a knee right now and I might seriously welcome a heart attack. I pushed my body to the limit and kept running until my lungs burned. Exhausted and feeling momentarily safe, I stopped, finding myself once more at the shores of the lake.

The sign in the grass behind me read "Loyola Park". I was standing in the sand while the cold water chillingly licked the shore. The baseball fields loomed in the distance and not having the energy to run anymore, I just stood there and admired the beautiful rhythm of the water. The cold breeze caressed my face; I gave into it and closed my eyes. I let it envelope me and dance around me. With my eyes closed, the lapping and crashing of the small waves became more intense, it was all I could hear. I tilted my head back and opened my eyes. The cold night's sky created a crisp canvas for the stars above. The distant stars and not so distant planets twinkled and flashed from above. I let the wind, the waves, and blazing distant suns take me. My feet started to move and I found myself surrounded by water at the edge of the pier.

I wasn't sure if it was the vodka still in my system, the amazing night, or my screwed up circumstances, but I felt finally at peace. The feeling warmed me to the core and made every hair follicle on by body stand at attention. Tears of joy started to stream down my face as I smiled up at the stars. I knew my time might be coming soon, but I had made a difference. What I would have given to be holding Lumi right that second.

The euphoria and melancholy faded as I started to hear footsteps approaching me on the pier. My smile faded and I quickly wiped away the tears from my face. The stars returned my eyes to me and as my head hung, now I could only see the concrete pier on which I stood. The waves kept dancing and crashing as the steps got louder. The footsteps stopped and a heavy destiny waited behind me.

The voice made the cools nights' breeze send a chill through my spine. "Glad you have finally accepted your destiny, Jordan. This is not a joyous occasion for me, but it must be done."

I had heard many times during my training and career the voice of the Auditor. The deep voice was always cold, menacing, and to the point. I recognized the voice coming from behind me very well, but there was emotion behind it now. It made it less threatening and made me feel bad for the Auditor in some twisted way. The voice had always been almost robotic with its menacing warning and training, but no more.

I took a deep breath, made peace with what was about to happen, and turned to see the face of my executioner. The voice always had carried so much weight and fear in all of us, since the only ones to ever get to see the face of the Auditor were those who were about to be dispatched. I slowly turned, expecting to see some horrifying mutation. Something, someone so gruesome that the only role they could find in Civilization's society was as the executioner and Auditor. My heart sped up and started to resonate inside my ear drums, the beating rhythmically intensifying the tension of the situation. I completed my turn and time stopped.

The sound of the waves disappeared, the wind stopped blowing, and everything went completely dark. An energy weapon was firmly pointed at me, held in a strong hand. My eyes refused to follow the arm up towards its owner. What stood before me was more grotesque and terrifying than anything I could have imagined. It didn't have horns. Its face wasn't morbidly deformed. The eyes were not two black pits staring back at me. Despite my most vivid fantasies of what the Auditor must look like, what stood before me surpassed them all. The eyes, the face, the hair flowing in the wind were more perfect and beautiful than I could have imagined. It was also frighteningly familiar. I had wished and wanted Lumi next to me in this moment and in this peaceful place. Instead, Lumi stood a few meters away from me, pointing the energy weapon at me and destroying my heart.

The tears began to flow again, born out of the most excruciating pain I had ever felt. The energy weapon had not discharged, but Lumi had already killed me. Every single thing I had done was so we could feel the love I saw in the Randoms. There was no other person, thing, or anything in my life more important than my Lumi. I had trusted Lumi with all of my being and heart and it was all about to be collected in pieces.

I hadn't realized, but my mouth had been hanging open as I tried to process the vision in front of me. I tried to speak, but my throat hurt as the tears madly escaped my eyes. I swallowed hard and I felt blades flowing down my throat, through my heart and all over my body. When I had composed myself from the recoiling and intense pain I was in, I said the only thing my trembling lips allowed me to emote.

"But I love you..." I wanted to say so much more. I had so many questions I needed answered, but my body would not cooperate. I fell to my knees and the tears became sobs. The cold concrete felt extra solid underneath my knees. I knelt looking at the still drawn weapon facing in my direction. Lumi's eyes were beautiful as ever, but were cold and devoid of any emotions. I searched for any sign of love and compassion, but found none. Had it all been a lie? Every kiss and every day we had; had it all been a mission for Lumi? The more I asked myself, the more the possible answers broke me inside.

The pain grew every second until I was eager to welcome an energy blast right through my chest. I desperately awaited death and the end of the charade my life had been. I had expected this day to come, but never like this and never by Lumi. I raised my arms as if to ask why, but my mouth once more failed. Snot was freely dripping out of my nose blending with the tears, tasting of a salty misery.

The waves seemed to be raging now and the wind howling in anticipation of my execution. Lumi's arm came down to a rest, still firmly holding the energy weapon. For a second I could swear Lumi's eyes softened or maybe I had just imagined it. An energy blasted through the dark night barely missing Lumi. Lumi's attention went from me to where the blast had come from. I took the mysterious rescuer blast, along with Lumi's momentary softness towards me, as a sign and made my escape. I lunged into the cold waters and began to swim deep into the lake.

The coldness of the water compressed every molecule of air out of me, but I didn't have time to dwell. I swam as fast and as hard as I could away from the barrage of energy blasts. With every stroke my body warmed and

I was able to breathe a little easier. I didn't dare look back at what was going on back at the beach. I swam until all I could hear was the ever present dance of the lake's water. I stopped my frantic swimming and just treaded water. I turned, trying to see where I had come from shore, but all the shore was just but a distant postcard. The skyscrapers climbed into the skies in their dreams to touch the moon. The lights from shore flickered as magically as the ones from the stars above. I floated and took in the beauty of the city from out in the middle of the lake.

I felt completely alone and disconnected floating in the middle of the dark cold lake. I considered stopping my arms and feet and letting the infinite darkness of the depths collect me. Every single action I had taken in my adult life had been for nothing. What was the point of continuing to fight and swim? I wanted it all to end, I knew my mission had been an insignificant one in the grand scheme of the Universe, but I hadn't felt how insignificant until that moment.

I was ready to give up, so I did. My arms and legs stopped cutting through the water and my body slowly began to sink. I let the air escape my lungs for one last time through my nose, leaving a trail of bubbles as I sunk further into the infinite bottom of the lake. I kept looking up until the stars disappeared and I was completely engulfed by darkness. My heart first raced then slowly the beats came further and further apart. My eyes started to close and I could feel the nothingness ready to take me.

That is when the phrase popped in my head. "There are others." I could hear Mike's words saying it and the words echoed over and over inside my head. "There are others." I was broken, betrayed, and destroyed inside, but there were others. As I drifted in and out of consciousness, I realized it wasn't just my mission or fight. There were others clawing and scratching for the same purpose and goal I so furiously fought for. There are others who needed me and I was the only person alive to see and know who the Auditor was. As much as it broke my heart, that information was too valuable to sink into the depths with me.

My eyes opened and my lungs panicked. I started to kick and swim upwards following the distant trail of bubbles back to the surface. My lungs were burning and my body was moving on pure will. I climbed out of the hold of the lake and finally exited into the cold night air. I took a deep breath as I broke the surface and my lungs once more inflated. There are others. The words gave me purpose and resonated inside my heart and mind as I took every painful stroke back towards the shore.

I crawled onto shore exhausted and cold. I wanted to lay there my right cheek resting on the sand, but purpose flowed through my veins. I slowly found my way to my feet purely on will. I quickly surveyed the area and I was alone. I wasn't dealing with normal prey anymore, I needed to arm myself. I was sure I would not find another energy weapon in this time, but there were weapons a plenty. We were advanced, but not bulletproof by any means. Lumi, I clenched my jaw as the name crossed my mind, The Auditor, would be coming for me soon. Next time I was going to make sure I would be able to fire back.

I accessed my forearm console and figured I had about 18 kilometers to hike to properly arm myself. I didn't waste time; it was the middle of the night so the streets were mostly empty. I was in no shape for an all-out sprint, I didn't feel the need to run in normal human speed anymore. I ran through the quiet city driven by anger and the resolve that I would not die in the hands of the Auditor.

The sporting goods store was large and secure with rudimentary technology. I made haste and found the weapons department. I was a bit overwhelmed by the choices, but quickly decided on a few pieces and plenty of ammunition. Once properly geared up, I took some of the beef jerky packets in the box on the counter and started to make my way towards a park/cemetery I had noticed on the map just a couple of kilometers away. Someone was going to die tonight, might as well have it happen on "sacred" grounds.

I didn't feel the need to rush anymore. I was walking through suburbia and everyone was tucked in and asleep in their houses. The streets were completely empty and the only noise was the one of the dying leaves rustling in the wind up ahead. The fire and anger in me kept growing. I felt myself want to give into the pain, but kept feeding the raging fire of fury reminding myself that "there were others". Erasing Mr. Michelson had made enough waves through time. They were set on stopping me and I was going to make sure to keep the changes coming until I could call myself human again.

I first ran into the cemetery, the trees peppered in between the graves were almost bare. A few resilient leaves held on in the windy night. I could hear the river up ahead so I cut through the graveyard until I hit its embankment. Towards the north the trees became dense and the waving orange, red and brown leaves invited me to explore them. I headed north along the river and into the woods. It served both as shelter from the Auditor and kept any locals from witnessing what was about to happen.

The water danced opposite to my steps as I went up river. I walked under the overpass bridge and entered almost a mystical land. I was no longer surrounded by edifices of concrete. I was surrounded by life in its purest form. The trees were preparing for the winter and were half way through shedding their photosynthetic suits. The brown trunks leaned over the life giving river, protecting it from the night sky. It would be about a thousand years before humans discovered the true intelligence of plants and trees, but I could see it plain as day as I walked up the river.

I greeted them as I walked and bargained for help for what was about to come. I doubted they would act on my behalf, but it didn't hurt to ask. I looked at my forearm controls and was tempted to send out a beacon signal so the Auditor would find me and we could get this over with. Instead, I realized I needed to send a message to warn the village about what had happened. I wasn't sure how, but I was pretty sure I could figure out how to send message to Martina, she was a smart girl, she would figure out how to receive it.

I tinkered with controls until I was able to figure out how to send a short recording to Martina. I knew the temporal and geographical coordinates, I just didn't know to what device I was sending it. I was banking on one of the many toys she had in her building picking it up. They needed to know who the Auditor really was. Everything I had done paled in comparison to what that tiny bit of information really meant. When I finally looked up from my forearm controls I could see the first few hues of orange and pink peeking above the trees. I had spent a few hours figuring it out and had totally lost track of time.

I had found some comfort sitting on the leaf littered ground and resting against a fallen tree. Drained and devoid of any adrenaline, my breathing slowed and my chest became heavy. My eyes kept admiring the beautiful explosion of fire that was breaking the horizon. The leaves came to life and matched the blazing colors of the sky. The calm flow of the river soothed me as my eyes became heavy and unable to fight it; I gave in to the peacefulness of sleep.

Quiet, but telling footsteps through the sea of dead leaves woke me from my slumber. The sun was out now, but the sky was still ablaze with oranges, reds, and yellows. I quickly reached for my commandeered shotgun and had my eyes listen to my ears. I scanned attentively the area where the last rustling of leaves had come from, but it was all quiet now. I stayed alert and focused on letting my ears explore the woods for my hunter.

Once more the sneaky footsteps were given away by the death decaying on the ground. I turned to my left, finger poised on the trigger of the rudimentary weapon and ready to fire the first shot. A mask wearing little thief looked back at me amused by my tactical moves. He stood there for a few seconds observing me as I slowly lowered my weapon. The grey and black night crawler studied me with an intelligence in his eyes few animals had. I could see the tiredness and exhaustion of a night marauding and pillaging in suburbia in the poor little critter's eyes. Satisfied with its observation of me, the raccoon turned and continued on his way towards its hidden borough. The rodent's feet made little crunchy sounds as it disappeared into the woods as stealthfully as it had once appeared.

I found myself smiling at the raccoon's ambivalence and amusement at my reaction. It knew something was happening, but it was inconsequential to him. So after it got it's fill of the silly "human", it went on its merry way. Footsteps crunching as they ran caught my attention once more. This time they were heavy and hurried footsteps. They got louder and more frantic as they approached me from my right. I readied the shotgun once more this time knowing that unless a bear was charging me it had to be the Auditor. I could hear the dead branches snapping off the trees as my new assailant didn't slow down for its own safety.

The crunching of the leaves and twigs on the ground grew deafening with every approaching step. My heart raced and pounded inside my chest and I did all I could to calm my breathing so I could steady my shot. I could start to a see shadow weave through the trees relentlessly approaching me. It was a large silhouette, not large enough for a bear, but definitely humanoid. I would not have a clear shot until the figure left the safety of the woods and entered the small clearing I had found residence in. I had no more than a few meters and the figure would be on me quickly. I stopped listening to the footsteps and focused my ears on searching for the indistinguishable sound of an energy weapon charging. My eyes had the rushing shadow covered; it was not up to my ears to figure out its intent.

I waited the last few seconds and the shadow finally broke into the clearing. Out of the woods, looking worse for wear, came Mike. He looked like hell and seemed desperate as he closed the last distance between us. His left arm just hung next to his body as he ran, dangling like a cooked noodle. The top of his left shoulder was scorched and burned with his shirt melted into his skin. The burnt and scarred tissue extended up his neck, finishing on his head which now was missing most of the hair on his left side. What was left was singed, matted, and covered with blood and other liquids. I lowered my weapon and readied myself to catch the desperate and wounded man.

He tried to slow down, but his momentum made his battered body crash into me. He made a small whimpering sound as his body collided into mine. I caught the injured man and slowly lowered him to the ground. I set him resting against the fallen tree where I had just taken my short nap prior to being awakened by the masked bandit raccoon. He winced and protested every step of the way. Once on the ground and after a few deep breathes, Mike steadied himself and proceeded to grab my left wrist where my forearm controls where located. I quickly pulled my arm away, partially out of reflex, and partly because of his frenzied look.

"What are you doing, Mike? What happened?" I prompted the heap of a man, my eyes going back and forth between my forearm controls and him.

"The Auditor happened, that is what! I need to send a message back and you are my only link. I don't have much time, I can feel my body starting to shut down and I am afraid I am too far gone to be saved. I need to get a message back to Abemi."

Mike was keeping himself under control, but the panic was starting to burst through his worn seams. I wanted to explain to him I had already sent a message, but before I could get a word out he reached and grabbed my left arm again. I didn't fight it this time and allowed the dying man to do what he must. I watched as he could barely hold his body up against the dead tree, but his one functioning arm furiously worked on the console. He accessed bandwidths and entered commands I had never seen in all my decades of dealing with my control. His fingers slowed down as he entered the last few strokes. His right index finger hovered over the display ready to hit the execute command, but he stopped. He looked back at me and tears were running down his charred and scarred face.

"I am sorry, Jordan." Before I could see his tears and the guilt in his eyes, his finger stroked the last command. I felt the world disappearing on me and commencing my plummet through the time-stream wormhole. Every second of the mind bending trip was filled with excruciating pain. There were no dampers and no safeties. I was experiencing time travel like the first explorers did, most of which either died or ended up insane. My jaw clenched as I felt the increasing and every changing forces pressing on my body. I closed my eyes for they felt they might pop out of my head in the rapid cycling between overwhelming pressures and vacuums. I could feel my skin barely hanging on to the flesh underneath it and at that moment my muscles began to spasm uncontrollably everywhere in my body.

The endless torture abruptly ended and for the one second I could perceive, I could tell I was back in the Lake Umatilla village. After my one quick second of perception, the world went to static. My eyes were overtaken by brightness and all I could see was wide blinding and painful light. It was like staring into pure whiteness and the endlessness of it reaching back and stabbing me in the eyes. My ears began to ring, every second the ringing became louder and higher pitched. My hands reached to the side of my head as the high pitched noise wanted to make me claw my ears out of my cranium. My stomach joined the full body revolution and I started to vomit uncontrollably. It would not stop and the stomach acid burned as it came out. My lungs struggled to breath; shallow gulps of air were the only thing keeping me from asphyxiating from the spasms that had overtaken my body. I convulsed and seized on the ground aware of what was going on, experiencing every nanosecond of misery, but unable to stop it or do anything about it. The agony intensified and I felt myself going mad. It was relentless and unstoppable, my body had experienced something no human was ever meant to endure and live. Aware of my impossible situation, I felt my body start to shut down between the convulsions and excruciating pain. With no other option in my impossible reality, I gave in to my only salvation and embraced death.

TRUTH AWAKENS

My eyes slowly opened. Everything was a blur and I was too weak to even panic. I kept gently blinking and the room started to come into focus. I tried to open my mouth, but my lips had crusted shut together. I tried harder until my jaw was able to stretch and part them. My lips, now opened, stung from being forcibly separated. The little bit of pain finished bringing my vision into focus.

It took all the energy I had just to turn my head in the bed and take the whole room in. Small tubes stuck out of my left arm, they led up to a machine which was pumping liquids from the different bags hanging from it. I tried to move my arms, but all I could manage was a small quiver out of them. The room was bare, with only the apparatus flanking each side of the bed to decorate. There were a couple of bright lights hanging from the dark ceiling. The walls were made of rock and looked almost moist in appearance. There was no fourth wall and out of the room I could just see a corridor of rock. The room looked like a small pocket was carved into wet moist grey rock. This was a strange looking place for being the afterlife. Good thing I didn't believe in such nonsense.

A surprised Random turned the corner. The lady's white face turned even paler. Her eyes widened as she saw me looking back at her, accompanied with a little hop to stop her forward steps. She looked at me one more time to make sure it wasn't her imagination, then she turned back into the stone hallway screaming. "It's awake, it's awake." The amusement at her surprised, scared face quickly disappeared after being referred to as an "It". The word hurt me, I was an enigma lost in the ambiguous perfect limbo we had created as a species. I should have been proud to be the apex of evolution and technology. Instead I felt lost and confused. That void of knowing what and who I was drove me to the Randoms as a youngster. I have been on the search to define who I was ever since. I thought I had made progress, but that simple word made my heart weep.

A familiar and friendly face came around the cold and heartless stone. Abemi approached me smiling from ear to ear. Her hands came together over her mouth as she walked and I could see the beginning of tears starting to well up in her eyes. She quickly got next to the bed where I was worthlessly laying and quickly grabbed my right hand. She held my hand inside hers, I could see it with my eyes, but my hand was having a different experience. Her hands felt like a distant and dying echo wrapped around mine. The feeling was so faint I didn't know if it was real or being imposed on my hands by my eyes.

I struggled to speak, but my body refused my brain's commands. Abemi, noticing my struggle, quickly hushed me and planted one finger over my mouth. "Just rest Jordan, just rest." Abemi's caramel voice made my straining body relax. She nodded to the jittery nurse at our side, her smile momentarily disappearing. Abemi turned her dark brown, almost black eyes, back to me and continued to comfort me with her kind expressions. The nurse jumped at her look and disappeared to my left. Abemi kept repeating that I needed rest, soon a chemical wave of relaxation flowed through my body. I could feel the calmness spreading through my limbs and my eyes getting heavy. I blinked a few more times and Abemi disappeared and was replaced by the darkness of slumber.

This cycle continued, every time I would wake up Abemi would be there. Every time I had a little more strength, but wasn't able to talk yet and every time the nurse would send me back to slumber. I lost count of how many times it happened, but it was more than twenty. I knew I needed the rest, but it was very frustrating not knowing what happened, where I was, and being there were no windows in my stone room, how many days had passed.

I stopped fighting it each time and waited until I could not only talk, but could prevent the nurse from giving me whatever anesthetic cocktail that she was giving me. I rested and I felt better each time I woke. I waited patiently, then I finally made my move. I opened my eyes and saw the nurse and Abemi on her chair. She quickly stood, smiling and coming over to comfort me. She grabbed my hand as that was her usual routine now and I could feel every centimeter of her embrace. Once more Abemi urged me to sleep and rest. She nodded to the nurse and as the nurse tried to move around my left flank, I surprised her.

"Stop! No more." I turned and pointed at the poor nurse as I said it. She jumped about a meter back and let out a loud screaming yelp of surprise. She stood there paralyzed, and I turned my attention back to Abemi.

"I am well enough and I am tired of resting in this bed. Where am I, how did I end up here, and what happened?" Abemi held strong, but her expression was invaded by sorrowful eyes. She started to nod, every movement of her head more pronounced each time. She puckered her lips and let out a big sigh. "Ok, Jordan, ok."

She once more made a gesture to the paralyzed nurse, who scurried out of the room's opening. She quickly returned with a wheelchair in tow. She parked it next to the bed and hesitantly approached me. Abemi's hand invitingly pointed to the wheelchair. "Let's go for a stroll, Jordan. I will catch you up with what has been going on." I wanted to protest the wheelchair, but the promise of information was too compelling and truthfully, I wasn't sure if I could walk or not yet. I shooed away any sort of help and got myself into the wheelchair. Abemi grabbed the handles in the back and away we went for out little chat.

We exited the hospital room just to be welcomed by an even stranger looking hallway. The wall and the ceiling, if you could call them that, were but a tunnel carved out of the same dark grey rock which surrounded me in the room. Lights were strung along the top of the tunnel illuminating our way. Cables and pipes ran along the ceiling making them look like giant worms. We passed several Randoms while she walked and I rolled, all of them stopped to give us way. They all looked at Abemi with great respect and at me with a bit of fear. The once friendly and inviting Randoms were now replaced, by anxious, stressed, and agitated looking ones. I soaked in every little detail I could, but wasn't able to make many deductions, I just had more questions for my wheelchair driver.

We twisted and turned through the everlasting stone hallways and I wondered if we had a destination as Abemi kept pushing me along. Finally we reached what looked like a dead end, guarded by four mountainous men. Their large muscular bodies were covered with weapons of all different sorts, explosives, guns, and even knives adorned their corpulent torsos. Their arms lay mostly bare. Apparently, no piece of clothing was fitting or strong enough to go over their swollen arms. The grip on their weapons tightened as we approached and their bodies tensed in attention towards Abemi. The muscles on their arms rippled through the overstretched thick skin, making their veins protrude, making their arms look like ancient maps.

"Please open it." Abemi's words startled me. I had forgotten she was still there while I was entranced with the four large centurions. They all nodded, put down the weapons, and began to press on the stone wall behind them. At first the wall didn't yield, but as their muscles became engorged with blood under their skin the wall slowly began to move. Every step they took was laborious and I could hear them hiss air in and out of their burning lungs as they moved. Slowly the wall moved, but I couldn't see anything beyond it from my movable chair.

After a couple of meters, a loud click resonated through the corridor and the huffing and puffing of the mountains of muscles stopped. They all walked back now, covered in beads of sweat, and picked up their weapons. Abemi grabbed onto the handles on the wheelchair and pushed me out the small opening the muscle quartet opened for us.

I expected to be blinded by the sun as we exited, but it was night time. Only the gentle twinkle of the stars welcomed my eyes. The full moon danced in the clear night illuminating the mountainside. In the distance, a sprawling metropolis stood before us. It looked familiar, but I couldn't quite make out what it was. Abemi stopped rolling me along as the loud click once more filled the night's air and the side of the mountain retracted back, sealing the opening. She came around and stood next to me, her eyes staring out into the distant city. I sat there in silence as she looked like she was collecting her thoughts and waited for her to fill me in on what had happened.

After a few minutes, she finally broke the night's silence. "Michael sent you back. You barely made it, Jordan. You are the first person to withstand 4 jumps in that short of a period of time and you barely made it."

"Where is Michael?" I had almost forgotten about our last encounter in the woods of Chicago.

"He didn't make it. He was too injured to make the jump with you and the Auditor got a hold of him eventually, as the Auditor always does. He did send with you and your arm console a wealth of information that helped us immensely." I looked down at my left forearm just to discover it was wrapped in bandages. I reached with my right hand and was instantly greeted with shooting pain, after I poked where the console should have been.

"We had to remove it to make sure you could not be tracked here. This is our safe house and where we make our final stand, we could not risk being discovered."

I felt naked without my console and, to a certain extent, trapped. Abemi stood there quietly, so I decided it was time for me to get my questions answered. I wanted to ask patiently, but the anticipation overtook me. Question after question spilled out from my lips and into Abemi's ears. I hoped she remembered them all once I was done and I shut up to give her a chance to answer.

She finally broke the silence of the night. "This is the home of our last stand. What you see across the river in the distance is Seattle, one of the main metropolis for civilization. With the information Michael sent back, and everything within your arm console, we not only know who the Auditor is, but where to strike to overthrow Civilization's power. Like you Jordan, we want things to go back to the way nature intended. In our imperfection, we find true humanity. Civilization has robbed millions of that and we intend to stop it. Once you made it back, we had to move quickly. Our homes were quickly overrun and taken by Civilization's henchmen."

A shiver went through my body fearing the worst. I already had the blood of one village on my hands, I could not bear the thought of another. "We were able to escape and clear the village before they arrived. As they riffled through our homes and violated our lands, is when we first struck. Explosive after explosive leveled the village, along with one of Civilization's platoons."

I didn't know how to feel and the tone of joy in her voice made things deep inside my stomach twist. Abemi continued as her words took flight after remembering that first violent strike.

"Since then, we have strategically been coordinating attacks all over the continents. Every day, every hour, we deal great blows against Civilization's tyranny." She paused and looked at her wrist, which was adorned with a watch. "Strike like this." Her open palm directed my attention back to the distant city skyline. Even from the distance I could see small orange flash after small orange flash explode in the night sky. One of the larger buildings began to topple as a distant wisp of smoke began to reach up to the night's sky. I looked back towards Abemi in disbelief and horror.

"You have been recovering for 17 days Jordan, the world has greatly changed in that time. With your and Michael's intel, we have been able to strike at many strategic targets of KronoCorp. As you well suspected, KronoCorp is the true puppet master behind what humanity has become. The building you just saw collapse housed a great number of the workers of the KronoCorp operation in Seattle." Abemi's eyes turned to me filled with joy and madness. "Thanks to you, Jordan and the men and women who gave their lives to carry on these missions, and similar missions throughout the continent, we have more than halved KronoCorp workforce in North America and erased most of their board. This is one of the major strikes in taking our world back and I am happy and proud to stand next to you here as it happens."

I was truly at a loss for words. The kind gentle woman who I had first met was no more. Her eyes blazed with rage and blind passion. I had wanted to take the world back to what it should have been, but never this way, never this violently, and never at such a high cost. My gut twisted and made me worry about Lumi. Even though Lumi had turned out to be the most feared person in the world, I still loved and cared for Lumi. I worried that in tonight's explosive mission by the Randoms, my Lumi might have perished. I forced a smile and avoided Abemi's eyes, instead focusing on the changed skyline of the city across the water. There was no way my ears could hear the cries and screams of the panicked people, but my heart did and I dreaded what I helped start.

Abemi talked into a small black box she had been concealing and a response promptly came back. After a few seconds, the mountain opened up again allowing us sanctuary inside its rocky inners. The roll back to my hospital room was a quiet one. I could feel the excited energy of triumph emanating from Abemi as she led me through stone hallway after stone hallway. I sat quietly in horror as I felt I was being led not to my room, but to my prison cell. Once I was lying restfully back in my bed, my mind overwhelmed me with thoughts and undeniable guilt. I felt like a prisoner and a hostage. My arm console had given them access to information which was highly classified. I rubbed my forearm once more, missing my decade's long companion. The nurse reattached me to the bags of solutions hanging from the metal rod. I could tell she was going to put me under once more and after what I'd learned and witnessed, I didn't fight her. I embraced the restful darkness and part of me wished I would never wake up from it again.

I did wake up and even though I was feeling better, I would lay in bed waiting for the nurse to come back and put me under. Days passed and I continued to hide in my slumber. The nurse eventually protested, but I convinced and begged her to put me back under. Her surprised look was now replaced by pity and mercy. I lost track of days and time through my attempts at escaping reality. I kept wishing I wouldn't wake up every time, but reality kept pulling me back out.

As the many days prior I woke up from my chemically induced sleep, only to find the room empty and the nurse nowhere in sight. I started to reach for the call nurse button when the rocks around me shook. Little trails of dirt and dust sprinkled from the almost invisible cracks on the dark grey rocks around me. I could hear agitated voices and shouting coming from the hallway. Again the tunnels shook and I decided to get up from the bed which had housed me for weeks.

A few flashes of urgently moving people could be seen through the door-less opening to the room. I riffled through the small dresser next to the bed and found some clothing and surprisingly a gas mask. I quickly changed out of the gown I had been wearing. I didn't quite feel like running around showing my ass to everyone in the middle of whatever chaos was happening.

I carefully approached the opening out into the hallway, getting in better earshot of the voices. I listened intently and was floored by what I heard. I knew right that second I had to escape and that this might be my only chance. I carefully tried to remember my little roll with Abemi. I had a couple of ideas of how I might be able to get out of here, but I needed to act fast. I put on the gasmask and excited into the hallways in search of my escape and salvation.

People where zooming back and forth through the hallways. Some of them were sporting the fashionable black gasmask like me. Most were carrying weapons and moving with a purpose. The secret lair of the Randoms had been discovered and all hell was breaking loose. I wasn't sure where I would go. I didn't have my arm console so I could not jump and heading back into KronoCorp would be suicide. I just knew I could not stay here anymore. I could not be part of what the Randoms had turned into. I had to flee and if the universe was kind to me, hopefully I would be mowed down in the firefight.

I walked through the hallways having to backtrack a few times, but I finally found the way out. I climbed the ladder until there were no more rungs. Above me stood a hatch with a handle on it. I had come this far, so I decided to give the handle a try, and hoped it would open. I turned it forcefully and was happily greeted with the click of the latch unlocking. I almost exploded out like a jack in a box, but decided otherwise. I could feel my heart racing in my chest. I had no idea of where I would go once I was out of wherever the hatch led. I took several deep breaths before I plunged into the unknown. I opened the small door, slowly peeking around before I exposed myself. Only green and plant life looked back at me and I felt a weight come off my shoulders. My desire to be gunned down and eliminated had suddenly disappeared and the urge to survive and keep fighting overwhelmingly took over.

Feeling as comfortable as I was going to get, I opened the hatch and exited into the dense woods. I closed the small door after me, just to see how it was perfectly camouflaged by its surroundings. The ground was pitched, telling me I was on the side of some sort of hill. The trees and shrubs obscuring my vision from venturing too far, clarified for me I was actually on the side of a mountain. There was really only one direction to pick, so I headed down. I moved at a quick pace, but remained vigilant of anyone or anything close by. In the far distance the faint sound of energy weapons and gunfire disturbed the otherwise tranquil setting.

I made quick work of the mountain and could only hear the fighting behind me. The noise of transports and carriers buzzed above me, but the canopy of the trees kept me hidden. I could see the trees starting to thin up, leading me into a clearing. Ahead of me stood a small meadow. Tall grass and flowers gently danced in the wind, impervious of the carnage going on further up the mountain. I had reached some sort of natural divide. Across from the small meadow and further down the mountain, another tree line began. The trees were thick, but looked different from the ones that currently gave me shelter. The meadow cut the two ecosystems in half and the only way for me to continue down the mountain was to expose myself while crossing through the dancing flowers. I caught my breath and carefully considered my next move.

I was completely spent. I was feeling better, but by no means well yet. The world kept swimming on me in waves. I had moved as fast as possible to avoid detection while escaping the Random's base, but now I was paying for it. A short dash of maybe 150 meters seemed like a marathon. I kept looking for other ways around the clearing, but to no avail. I could still hear the transports buzzing to and fro, it wouldn't take much to stop me. I was making my escape to… well to nowhere, I didn't know exactly where I was going, but I knew where I didn't want to be.

I waited for my vision to steady, took a deep breath, and made my run for it. I wasn't moving anywhere as fast as I could, but I was sure I could escape the detection of Randoms, my kind was another story. Every step felt as it were in slow motion as my feet crumpled down tall grass. The small white flowers became a blur of lines and the next tree line seemed to be running away from me. My ears caught the unique buzzing sound of a transport approaching and my racing heart wanted to explode. Adrenaline, which I thought I had exhausted, flowed through my veins and my joints protested. Fear-- the grand ol' motivator. I could feel things tearing in my body as I propelled myself forward towards the relative safety of the forest ahead.

The static buzz of the air grew ever louder and my stomach reacted to it with violent knots. The hair follicles all over my body stood at attention as they were being pulled towards the magnetic fields of the transport. My lungs burned as the trees finally became trees and no longer a forest. I dove with my last bit of energy into the safety of the trees as the transport began to crest over them. I hit the ground hard and far enough from the edge so as to not be detected. My face slammed into the pine scented floor, I tried to gather myself, but the assurance of temporary safety led to an adrenaline dump. My vision once more blurred and danced, mixing the browns and greens of the trees into a surrealistic mass. I could hear my heart beating through my veins as they rapidly expanded and contracted throughout my body. My eyes blinks became longer and longer until the buzz, the colors, and my heartbeat disappeared.

Acrobatic droplets of rain avoided the dense canopy to greet my face and welcomed me back to consciousness. The welcoming sounds of the rushing rain greeted me. I tried to move, but everything hurt. I had never felt like this before in my long life. The pain in my joints was overwhelming and made me get up to my feet laboriously. I held onto the tree next to me for support as I remembered how to stand and worked up the courage to walk. Anarchist droplets insisted on attacking my head. My feet shuffled me slowly away from the drops and under the canopy's full safety. I could see out to where the meadow should be, but a curtain of moving water obscured it. I felt safe in the blanket of the deluge, so I moved gingerly in between the trees. I used the big old trunks for support until the forest kindly provided an adequate walking stick.

I walked down the mountain slowly, without a real heading but down. I couldn't go back to the Randoms and who knew what kind of fate awaited me back in Civilization and KronoCorp. To say the least, I didn't hurry and spent the next three days wondering slowly, but surely down the mountains towards whatever was left of New Seattle.

As I got closer to the city, I could periodically hear distant explosions followed by the echoing reverberation of the emergency vehicle sirens. Whether I wanted to accept it or not, a civil war had broken out, the first one in over 3,000 years and I had a small part in it. Maybe a big part, I rather think I was just a small insignificant pawn in all of it, but my gut told me otherwise. Whatever my true involvement was, I needed to find where I fit in this chaos and more importantly, what I was going to do.

I spent a few days dancing around the edge of the city carefully, calculating rushing in for some food, just to return to the safety of the forest. I debated for how long I could do this dance. I knew it would only take a few moments for the grid to pick me up and let KronoCorp and my love, Lumi, know where I was.

Just thinking of Lumi made my eyes well up and my chest to hurt. I had spent every waking second keeping myself sane, thinking of what we would be once I was done with my mission. I wanted more than anything, to make love to Lumi; for the kisses, the caresses, and touches to actually lead somewhere, to feel true passion and love with my Lumi. In my fantasies, sometimes Lumi was my knight in shining armor, in others my beautiful bride. I truly didn't care what the ripples turned us into, as long as we were together. I remembered so many passionate kisses exchanged and how empty I felt at them being just kisses. I felt that Lumi was my true soul mate, but reality, ugly as it always is, played a cruel joke on me.

Why had Lumi allowed me so much leeway, knowing what I was doing, truly puzzled me? The Auditor should have eliminated me the moment any temporal transgression was committed, specially the kind I was perpetrating. I knew Lumi loved me, I felt it. Whatever was left in me that was truly human told me that Lumi did care about me and love me. It was the other 99.99% of me that feared and was certain that The Auditor would not miss again if given the chance to eliminate me.

I spent a few days doing my dance in and out of the city for food and provision. I was delaying the inevitable. As much as I respected and admired the Randoms, I was not a creature of the forest like them. The Randoms I knew were now gone, they had been gone since I was but a teenager. I had been chasing a dream, a nostalgic guilty memory which really didn't exist anymore. I knew that my green shelter was temporary. There was a date between me and my Lumi which I had to make. Maybe The Auditor would erase me or maybe my Lumi felt the same longing and need I experienced. It is hard to escape one's nature, but I could only hope.

I could have done this for an eternity, but that wasn't why I was here. I had worked my way over for days to the Eastern forest around the city. I decided to make my presence known at the shorelines of fall city. I wondered through the streets, working my way to its beautiful pier, and awaited my destiny.

I walked the city streets leaving the safety of the woods. I didn't hide my face and made a conscious effort for the cameras to see me. I expected a quick response team, followed by transports and The Auditor, to blitz me the second the cameras recognized me. Instead I walked through mostly empty streets in peace. I was both pleasantly surprised and disappointed at the lack of fireworks.

Frustrated, I kept walking and, spotting a security checkpoint, I hastened my pace. I could see the guards at the checkpoint starting to eyeball me as I closed the distance. Their attention was quickly averted from me as the ground shook. The light tremor was accompanied by a large distant explosion followed by one of the cylindrical skyscrapers tumbling down in the distance. They had to turn to see the scene, but it all unfolded slowly right in front of me.

The tall building was KronoCorp's headquarters in Seattle. The building had become a beautiful glass beacon and the symbol of the city. After the ground's first light rumble, the building started to collapse in the distance. Smoke, fire, and a larger tremor followed. My ears could not hear the screams, but my brain could. The Randoms had delivered a major blow to the infrastructure of KronoCorp and I didn't think the timing was coincidental. It was more blood on my hands and more souls to keep me up without sleep.

I kept walking. I wanted this to end, I needed this to end, and quickly. The guards at the checkpoint were already boarding the transport and heading to where they were needed. I walked past the now deserted post as I felt tears starting to stream down my face. My soul had broken with guilt and my feet carried me forward without instruction from my brain. Sirens could be heard near and far and the whole city mobilized itself against the strike from the Randoms. I continued my path to the docks and my damnation.

The tears didn't stop, even as my eyes gazed upon the dark expanse of the night's ocean. The distant stars blinked overhead as the moon made its final descent. It would be sunrise soon and I hoped to see it one last time. The panic and madness kept playing in the distance, but alone at the boardwalk, only the sound of the lapping waves accompanied me. There was not another soul in sight. I leaned on the railing listening to the relaxing waves, waited for the sun to rise, and wept like I never had.

The sun was glorious in its approach. Oranges, pinks, and reds danced over the mountains in the distance until the burning star eventually decided to show itself. The ocean went from black, to deep blue, to blue with little white caps to decorate it. The whole city was either in hiding or tending to the tragedy. The boardwalk was mine; the sun, the ocean, and the one lone figure standing in the distance. The small silhouette was more than a hundred meters away, but even from this far, I recognized it.

I had a sudden urge to flee and escape the destiny that lay in front of me. I forced myself to stand still and directed my eyes to where the once magnificent building had stood. Smoke billowed high into the sky like a ghost of the once proud building. I had done that, whether it was all me or not, I had a part in it, in all of this. My fists clenched, my jaw tightened, and I directed my eyes back to the now approaching figure and my destiny.

The fire that danced in the morning sky had been replaced with the purest and most intense cobalt I had ever seen. Never had a sky looked more vibrant and beautiful. The seagulls were out for their morning exercise, letting their presence be known, even though they rode the hot currents high above the ground. The ocean danced and the waves crashed on the piers of the boardwalk. There was a cool morning breeze which the sun was quickly warming up. Everything around me intensified and slowed down. I could feel, smell, and see things more intensely than I ever had. The figure growing on the boardwalk's horizon kept moving at the same pace though.

The distance evaporated and standing not two meters from me, was Lumi. My first urge was to run to Lumi and throw myself into an endless embrace. My lips burned with the desire to meet Lumi's. But my eyes quickly informed me that the figure standing in front of me was not the one I yearned for and remembered.

Lumi's eyes were tired and I could see the muscles flexing as the energy weapon hung from Lumi's right hand. The beautiful face, which I missed so much, had black soot over it and was decorated with new scars I had never seen. The usually spotless clothing looked like it desperately needed a wash. They were torn in places and the edges of the white shirt were stained with dry blood. Even the perfect hair was a mess. It was matted down with dark fluids in places, while it stuck up in attention in others. Once I soaked in the disheveled state of my usually sharp looking Lumi, I met the sad, tired, and angry gaze staring back at me.

The pain in Lumi's eyes was too much for me to be able to hold the gaze. I first looked down in shame and then turned to face the deep blue ocean next to me. I didn't know what to say. I stood there, my head turned looking into the infinity of the sea, and awaited for whatever Lumi, The Auditor, had in store for me.

"What have you done?" The words resonated through the empty boardwalk, bouncing back from the waves and echoing in my soul. My eyes closed as the pain of that question and my longing for Lumi's voice, hurt too much. I didn't know how to answer or what to say. Saying that I was sorry didn't seem adequate, so I gave the only answer I could, the only thing I could truly say.

"I… All… I love you and I fucked it all up." My voice was shaky and broken as I forced the few words out through my trembling lips. I looked into Lumi's beautiful eyes as tears blurred my vision and made the beautiful and broken specimen in front of me sparkle.

Lumi's hand relaxed on the weapon for a second, just to tense again as it was pointed at my chest. I dared not look away from those amazing eyes, for I wanted them to be the last thing I ever saw in my twisted existence. Lumi's arm hung there for what seemed like an eternity. The energy weapon began to tremble as the muscles holding it tired from pointing it at me for so long. I was glad it was going to be Lumi. I would go into the afterlife with his image burned into my retinas. It had been for Lumi that I had done everything I had. For our love, for the future I wanted us to have, and for what I needed us to be.

A loving smile formed on my trembling lips as tears parted around it. I would never be able to make love with Lumi, I would never have what the Randoms had with each other, it would never be the love stories from the past, but I loved Lumi with every cell of my being and every ounce of my soul. The being in front of me meant everything to me, for I had truly given everything up for Lumi. Giving my life would be but one last show of my love.

I could once again hear the ocean dance. The now warm breeze blew through my long hair, removing it from my face and caressing my skin. I could feel the sun shining down on me, warming my exhausted body, and giving it life. The waves gently crashed underneath our feet as the world dried my tears and calmed my soul. I could see Lumi clearly once more and the love of my life looked tired and broken, like I had never seen. It just made me love Lumi more. I took a deep breath and could smell Lumi's skin in the wind. My eyes closed for a second and my body reacted to the glorious scent. I opened my eyes and smiled once more at my Lumi. My mouth moved as my eyes opened into Lumi's, sharing my soul for one last time. I slowly nodded and smiled as I uttered the words Lumi needed to hear. The arm shook and Lumi fought to keep the energy weapon pointed at my chest.

"I love you Lumi and always will. It is ok."

Tears broke out of Lumi's usually collected eyes like I had never witnessed before. The hand trembled, not only from exhaustion, but from the sobbing and silent cries. The tears left little clean lines through the soot on Lumi's beautiful face. Lumi's lips trembled and the only way to stop them was to bite the lower one. The strong being I had loved and admired for decades disappeared and was replaced by a broken and conflicted one. I could see the pain in Lumi's eyes, as well as the love. This moment, this decision, was truly killing Lumi inside. I kept smiling and gently repeating over and over, "It's ok".

Lumi broke my gaze and stared upwards into the beautiful blue sky. I could see the ribcage expand and contract as Lumi took three deep breaths to get composed. Our eyes met once more and they were now dry. Lumi looked deep and long into my eyes and told me everything I ever needed and wanted to hear without uttering a word. The arm steadied the energy weapon as the warm ocean breeze danced in the space between us. Lumi took a step forward as one single tear escaped Lumi's left eye and told me exactly what I needed to hear.

"I love you, Jordan."

ABOUT THE AUTHOR

I am originally from Puerto Rico but have spent half of my life in the United States. My true passions are writing and cooking. My favorite authors include Edgar Allan Poe and Gabriel Garcia Marquez. From an early age I started writing poetry and short stories. My books are born out of the nightmares of my mind and melded with my life experiences. I would describe my books as reality sprinkled with a good magical dose of faerie dust. I hope my books can be entertaining but will also make the reader think.

37002864R00085

Made in the USA
Lexington, KY
19 April 2019